Midnight Blue

Nichole Ruschelle

Copyright © 2024 by Nichole Ruschelle

All rights reserved.

No part of this publication may be reproduced, distributed, or transmitted in any form or by any means, including photocopying, recording, or other electronic or mechanical methods, without the prior written permission of the publisher, except as permitted by U.S. copyright law. For permission requests, contact [include publisher/author contact info].

The story, all names, characters, and incidents portrayed in this production are fictitious. No identification with actual persons (living or deceased), places, buildings, and products is intended or should be inferred.

Cover Design by Opulent Designs

Photographer by Katie Cadwallader Photography, LLC

Editor: Utterly Unashamed

Proofread by: Megan Kelley

[Edition Number] edition [Year of Publication]

Contents

Dedication	V
1. Ella	1
2. Ella	11
3. Ella	17
4. Ella	25
5. Mikhail	36
6. Ella	47
7. Mikhail	50
8. Mikhail	55
9. Ella	61
10. Ella	65
11. Mikhail	71
12. Ella	79
13. Mikhail	86
14. Ella	94
15. Mikhail	101
16. Ella	110
17. Mikhail	115

18.	Mikhail	120
19.	Ella	129
20.	Ella	132
21.	Mikhail	138
22.	Ella	145
Epilogue		148
Also By Nichole Ruschelle		160
Acknowledgements		161
About the Author		163

To those who have always wanted to be daddy's baby girl.

One

Ella

My fingers lightly rub against the smooth paper. The words barely register in my mind. I can only focus on the elegant font and gold overlay. For a piece of paper, it's freaking gorgeous if not a bit ostentatious. But I guess that's the point. I found it while I was cleaning, shoved in the back of a kitchen drawer. I bet she thought I wouldn't find it there, but she should know better than that. It's obvious that they don't want me there. They like to keep me hidden. Out of sight, out of mind. Never would they take me to something fancy where the world might find out what they're like when people aren't watching.

My eyes scan the words once more, burning them into my brain. Memorizing every word like they might change as I read them.

> Thomas Family
> You are cordially invited to a masquerade ball
> to celebrate the opening of Midnight Blue.
> 9 pm - Black Tie Affair
> Masks are required at all times
> RSVP to parties@midnightblue.com

My hands sting as the invitation is ripped from them, leaving small paper cuts along my fingers. I don't look down at my fingers because it's useless. Instead I spin around quickly to find Mia standing in front of me with a scowl on her face.

"Why the fuck do you have this?" she yells harshly as she holds the paper up in the air.

I see something deep in her eyes, but I'm not sure what it is. I can't seem to put my finger on it. Her hands are twitchy as they hang by her sides with the invitation in one hand, and her face has turned pale. She has to be hiding something. Narrowing my eyes, I search her face looking for any indication of what it could be.

I want to know what it is.

I need to know.

Luckily she's easy to get information from. I just have to be careful how I extract it from her. I can't have her tattling to "Mommy." Throwing my hands on my hips, I snap back at her, "What's it for, Mia?"

Her lips go into a tight line. Folding the invitation, she places it in her back pocket and shakes her head. "It doesn't matter," she says in an uncharacteristically calm voice as she turns her body away from me.

Shit, I need to act fast to get more information from her. I can't let her walk away without finding out why they don't want me to know about the invitation. I rush out the same question as before. "Mia, what is the invitation for?"

Stopping in her tracks, she looks over her shoulder and rolls her eyes. "You don't need to know, because you won't be attending."

She's definitely hiding something. Her normal self would've bragged about an exclusive party. She would've thrown the fact that I wasn't invited in my face. Mia never wastes a moment to remind me that my place is beneath hers.

Taking a deep breath, because it's imperative that I stay calm and steady, I look her in the eyes making sure she understands me. "If I want to attend, I will. The invitation is addressed to the whole family and the last time I checked Mia, I'm still a part of this family."

Mia lets out an annoyed sigh like I can't possibly understand anything. "Ella, this is an important event. We don't need the riffraff of the family there. And on top of that even if you could go, you have nothing to wear and no money to buy anything."

Ignoring the jab she threw at me, I hold my armor in place not letting her see how her words hurt me. Over the years, I've become good at hiding my feelings. I learned at a young age that these people aren't my family, at least not in any way that counts. They don't care about me, and even though my brain knows this, my heart still yearns for the family we could've been.

"Mia, even if you don't want me there, I still have the right. I'm a part of this family."

"Ella, this party is for Mother to find us our husbands. You don't need one, so you don't need to go. Just stick with what you're good at, working on your knees. You're an independent woman, right? Even if you wanted a man, he wouldn't be a socialite from the likes of this event."

She throws her insults at me so easily, making it sound like I'm a whore when in reality I've only been with a couple guys who I met while bartending.

"The ball is to find a husband?" I ask in disbelief.

"Yes, Mother says everyone worth anything will be there," she replies with a wink.

Of course my step-mother plans to marry her daughters off for money. I guess that shouldn't surprise me. Not wanting to let my disappointment shine through, I give her what she wants. "Well, I could care less so you don't have to worry about me being there." I wave her off as I turn my back and leave the room.

If I keep asking questions she'll get suspicious, and the spoiled brat will tattle to her mother. But I smile to myself already planning.

I need to be there.
I will be there.
But no one can know.

If my step-mother finds out my plans, she'll punish me. Probably harsher than she has in the past. I shiver at the thought. I should disappear, leave all of this behind. But I won't. I'll endure what I need to because I won't leave my dad or lose my mother's house.

My phone vibrates in my hand, interrupting my thoughts. A small smile graces my lips when I see my best friend Suri's name.

> **Suri:** Hey, I'm home, but of course, the king and his witch aren't here.

> **Me:** Glad you made it home safely. It's probably for the best that the witch isn't there. Where did they go?

> **Suri:** True. They are staying in the city for the night. I'm going to take advantage of them being gone by catching up on Netflix. Do you want to come over and hang out?

> **Me:** I wish I could, but I have to work.
>
> **Suri:** That sucks. Maybe another time. Love you, have a good night.
>
> **Me:** Love you!

I walk in my room, a space that looks more like a storage closet than anything else. Boxes line the walls, full of my stuff. Stuff connected to memories from what feels like a past life. A life full of lightness, love, and laughter. A life where I didn't have to worry about surviving.

I used to have a big room upstairs that my mom had decorated just for me when I was younger. She took time to make sure that the room held all of my favorites, even down to the purple frames that held pictures of her and my father. Fairy statues lined my bookshelves along with her collection of classic books. Fairy lights hung across the ceiling above the bed and lace curtains lined the windows giving the room a light and airy feel.

The day that my father was admitted to the hospital after his cancer took a turn for the worse, I came home after sitting by my father's bedside all day to everything boxed up and moved to my current closet-like room. I tried to say something but they acted as if it was just stuff and not items that hold memories of the only woman who loved me.

Shaking off the melancholy feeling that always comes when I think about my past, I push through the boxes that engulf my room and grab my uniform for work off the top of the small chest of drawers.

Undressing, I look at myself in the one small mirror I have. I can't look for long. I don't want to see what I've become. My brown eyes have dark purple circles underneath them and they've lost their shine.

My body has taken a beating and not necessarily the kind you can see from the outside. It's the kind that lives in your heart and in your mind. The amount of stress that weighs me down, defending myself constantly from the anger that is thrown my way. It pushes me past my limits. My body is slowly disappearing. When I do want to eat, which isn't often, I can't because the step-monsters usually eat all of my groceries. These days I shove food down my throat in between shifts at the bar.

Mom died when I was ten and Dad decided he needed help raising me—and not a nanny…a new mom. He went on a few blind dates until he met my step-mother and her hideous daughters. Three months later, they were married.

At first when they came to live with us, I was excited to have siblings. I had always wanted sisters. But I quickly learned that these girls didn't want to be my sister. They wanted someone to berate. Someone to do their chores. They wanted me to know that I was beneath them.

In front of my dad, they treated me so nicely it was sickening, but as soon as he turned his back they would go back to their evil selves. Pushing me, stealing my stuff and hiding it, and making up rumors they would spread at school.

My step-mother never showed any feelings toward me. She wasn't rude or loving. It was like I didn't exist. Once my dad became sick about five years ago, she decided to notice me. And that was worse. Now she encourages her girls to put me down and she takes everything that means something to me.

So I survive and just try to get through each day, working to make enough money to buy this house before my dad dies. Before she can convince the lawyers that she should get the house instead. I know she won't care that his will names me as the beneficiary of the house. All she cares about is what she can get. But if I buy the house before he dies, then it doesn't matter what she thinks. I can kick them out and get on with my life. But all of that seems impossible.

Like I'm living in a horrible nightmare with no fairy tale ending in sight.

My phone alarm goes off, reminding me that I need to get going. Quickly I pull a tight, black body suit up over my torso followed by my tight skinny jeans. Turning around I glance at the mirror to check out my ass. Yep, these are the ones that should get me some extra tips.

Running to the bathroom, I line my eyes with black liner that makes my blue eyes pop. I coat my long lashes with mascara and I gloss my lips, smacking them. Perfect!

Dashing back to my room, I grab my keys and wallet, shoving them into my pockets as I glance at the time. Shit, I need to be at work in ten minutes. I shove my feet into my shoes and run toward the train stop, praying I make it in time.

When I scoot through the sliding doors, I drop down in the nearest seat. I place my hand on my chest and try to catch my breath.

"I made it."

A few stops later, I get off and briskly walk through the back door of the bar where I work, The Tower. Taking a deep breath, I relax and get my game face on, ready to work.

"That was close," a soft voice from my right says.

"It sure was. How is it out there tonight, Amber?" I ask her as I shove my keys and wallet into my locker, grabbing my apron and tying it around my waist.

"Not too bad. It hasn't gotten too busy yet."

"Well, I need it to get really busy. I need the tips."

Her face softens when I look over at her. "Your step-mom asking for more money?"

"Not yet. Just the usual expenses right now."

Amber sidles up next to me and throws her arms around my shoulders, crushing me into a side hug. "Don't worry. I'll make sure you're on the schedule, lots."

Laughing, I shrug her off. "Thanks, Amber. It helps that I'm the best bartender too, right?"

She chuckles, moving to the door that leads to the club and looking over her shoulder. "I didn't say that it wouldn't benefit me too. Now get your sexy ass out there."

Two

Ella

"Shit, my feet hurt," I whine under my breath as I balance against the bar while I lift each foot up trying to relieve the pressure. I know better than this, I internally scold myself. These shoes can't withstand hours at the bar on my feet. But I can't help but wear them. These bad boys make my butt look really good. And god knows I need those tips.

Tonight the bar is packed. I love it when it's busy. It stops me from thinking too much. Thinking about how my life is not what I expected it to be. How my dad is in the hospital on his deathbed and my step-mother and step-sisters still hate my guts. I drown myself in work so I can breathe.

A feeling of relief comes over me when I see the tip jar. My fingers twitch, wanting to count the money, wanting to reassure myself that everything is going to be okay at least in the short run. I hope it will be enough to pay the mortgage for the house this month. Since my father hasn't officially given the house to my step-mother she refuses to pay, leaving the responsibility to me. I keep staring at the jar, hoping that the amount will ease the pressure in my chest.

I just want to count it right now, but I can't. We don't count until everyone finishes their duties. Bar rules since we share the tips.

Time to finish closing up the bar. Thinking about my checklist for tonight, I grab the wet rag and start wiping down the bar. Amber approaches with a grin "Hey, how did you do tonight?"

I look back over at the tip jar then return back to her. "We haven't counted it yet, since we're not done with closing duties. But it looks like I did pretty good."

She goes and grabs the tip jar smiling, "Good thing I'm the manager and can count the tips myself."

"You are ridiculous," I tell her as I continue cleaning.

She lets out a screech of glee. "Ella, your cut from the tips is $1,000."

"No way. That can't be"

She hands me the pile of cash. I grab it cautiously, staring at it. Shit, this plus last night will be enough for the mortgage this month. Which means I can put my paycheck toward my savings to help me to buy the house.

Amber interrupts me by asking. "Will it be enough? Or do I need to put you on the schedule every night?"

Grinning like a Cheshire cat, I answer her "With these tips plus what I've already saved, it's enough. Thank god. But you know I'm already here every night. If it wasn't for you though, I wouldn't have made this many tips. We've never had this many customers. I bet Max is happy that he hired you as manager."

Amber ignores my comment about Max. For some reason they get along in a professional manner, but she refuses to speak about him. It's none of my business so I let it go.

Her eyes soften a bit as she leans over whispering to me "You know you can always strip. There's no shame in doing whatever you need to do to get by."

She points over to the other section of the bar and my eyes follow her finger. "Those girls make bank. You would be able to purchase your father's house faster. Sometimes I even think about giving up my manager position and going back to stripping."

Twiddling my fingers together, I answer, "I know, but if the step-witches found out, they'd humiliate me more than they already do. They would use it against me like stones to throw at a public shaming."

She swallows so hard I can hear it over the music, "I guess in this situation, it pays not to have any family then, huh?"

Holding back tears, I say, "In some ways, I can see the appeal, but I wouldn't trade the memories of my mom and dad for anything."

Turning away from her so she doesn't see how much her words affect me, I start straightening up the bottles of booze to give my hands something to do.

"Well, that was a little too deep for my liking," Amber chuckles and I'm thankful she broke up the emotional tension.

I glance at her over my shoulder with a smirk. She always knows how to lighten up the mood. "You know I found an invitation to the masquerade ball for the new club Midnight Blue in my kitchen drawer today?"

"No way! I've heard that freaky things happen at the masquerade ball. You should go."

"What do you mean 'freaky things' happen there? Have you been before?" I ask, using my free hand to provide the air quotes.

"Clients have come in and whispered that the nightclub is actually a front for a sex club. Only the elite are invited there for any events. Rumor has it the guy who owns the club is a total sex *god* but most people also think he's the heir of the Russian Bratva."

My jaw literally drops to the ground, then I let out a soft laugh. "No way. That sounds absurd." I wave my hand dismissing the rumors. "Mia, Leah, and my step-mother are planning to find husbands at the masquerade ball. I guess the elite part checks out, because they are total gold diggers. But I can't see them conspiring with dangerous people."

Amber slaps the bar, causing me to jump while I replay the conversation from earlier with Mia in my mind. "I meant it when I said that you should go."

Shaking my head no, I tell her, "They don't want me there... actually they forbid it." Softening my voice making sure it's gentle but direct to get my point across, I whisper, "She would punish me, Amber, if any of them saw me there."

Amber squeezes my hand giving me a bit of comfort before she lets go. With a huge mischievous grin, she says, "Knowing that, you have to go. Maybe you'll be able to get some blackmail material. Or maybe...just maybe...you'll get to have some fun for a change."

Without taking a breath, she continues, "Come by the bar first, I will take care of everything. Trust me they will never know you're there."

I relent, knowing that she's not going to drop this if I don't agree. "Fine, I'll go! But I'm only going to find out what they are up to."

Shrugging, she says, "Sure. But just promise me if possible you will let go a little, Ella. Have some fun?"

I can't promise her that so I don't respond. I wouldn't even know how to have fun. Moving away from her and hoping that she will drop it, I grab the rag back off the bar and continue wiping it down. Thankfully, she takes the hint and leaves me to finish up.

Entering the locker room, I can't help but feel excited when I look down at the pile of cash in my hand. I'm so excited to be able to pay the mortgage and put money away this month. Tonight I got one step closer to securing the house and making sure I keep one of the biggest memories of the family I no longer have.

Grabbing my bag, I head back out into the night. I hustle to the station to make sure I make the last train. I take a deep breath, taking in the smell of the city. My brain drifts back to the conversation with Amber about going to the masquerade ball. I just hope that she's right and I can get in without anyone noticing me. Call it women's intuition if you will, but I know they're hiding something from me.

Three

Ella

Waking up with a jolt, I frantically look around my room. I hear murmuring in the distance. "What the hell is going on?" I ask the empty room as I start to sit up in bed.

Through the thin walls, I can hear shouting between my step-sisters, Mia and Leah, as they argue over a dress. I roll my eyes at their antics and throw myself back onto the bed. Ugh…How is this my life?

"It's too damn early," I mutter while pulling the covers over my face, trying to hide from everything. I would love to just have one morning when they don't wake me up with their nonsense.

As the shouting dwindles down, my eyes flutter closed as my body tries to take me back into dreamland. But…no. Instead, my door bangs open, bouncing off the wall, making me quickly sit up in bed. My eyes settle on the silhouette in the doorway, the ice queen herself.

What could she possibly want? Why come all the way up to the attic, to my small closet? Usually she just sends my step-sisters to force me to do her bidding. But my step-mother in the attic...this can't be good.

Both of us stay exactly where we are, not moving, just staring at each other for what feels like forever. But I won't break first. I can't be the one that shows any weakness. I have to show strength at all times, no matter how much I want to fall apart. Rolling her eyes at me, she breaks the silence first with an eerily calm voice. "Ella, it's time to get Leah and Mia ready. We have an important dinner tonight."

I don't answer her, knowing it drives her crazy when I don't respond. I can't stop myself from pushing her boundaries even though I know it only makes my life harder. I do it any time I can, despite the punishments she loves to dole out. I don't have control of much in my life at the moment. This tiny act of defiance gives me just a little and I like the feeling it gives me. I maintain my silence, pushing harder by staring. Not breaking eye contact. After a few seconds, her tone becomes even sharper. "Get your lazy ass up, girl! I will not have you ruin this for us."

I try not to smirk. Her sharp tone gives her away. I hit the mark that I was looking for, but I don't want to push it any farther. I throw the covers off of the bed and start to get dressed. Still not bothering to acknowledge her. When she feels content that I'm following her orders, she turns and walks away. The farther away she gets from my room, the warmer it gets, finally allowing me a moment to breathe.

Our conversation starts to consume my brain and I can't help but wonder what she meant by ruining this for us? Even for her, she seemed more frazzled and on edge. I have that niggling feeling again. Something more is going on than just a dinner and masquerade ball.

And that can't be good.

So many questions are swimming in my head. I sigh dejectedly, knowing there's no point in dwelling because I'm not going to have the answers any time soon.

Except that's not completely true. Amber had the answer to my problem. I just have to be brave. Determination flows through my body. I'm going to find out what they're hiding no matter what.

I'm going to that ball.

In my small closet, I throw on a pair of jeans and an old T-shirt. I pull my hair up into a ponytail and head downstairs to the hall bathroom to finish getting ready. Then I make my way to my step-sisters' wing, ready to face whatever they throw at me.

Neither of them address me when I walk into their room, they just start giving out orders. I can tell today is not going to be easy, but it doesn't matter. I can take it. I'm used to it.

"Ella, I need you to launder these items before tonight," Mia barks.

As she shoves a few dresses at my chest, she continues talking and pointing her finger at me. "And you need to grab my jewelry that was cleaned last week."

Before she even finishes, Leah jumps in, throwing her own clothes on top of the pile, softly asking, "Ella, can you sew the strap back on this dress and launder it? When you get back from Mia's errand, I would love it if you could do my hair and makeup, too."

I've learned over the years not to argue, it's pointless. When I argue things get worse. Honestly doing their laundry and running errands is nothing. This is easy stuff compared to some of their other demands. I throw the items that need to be cleaned in the washer, grab my sewing kit, and start on Leah's dress.

I straighten out the dress on the bed assessing the best way to fix it. Thankfully, it will only take a few stitches. Super easy. In a couple minutes, I've reattached the strap without it being a noticeable fix and without causing any bunching of the surrounding material. I learned the hard way that Leah will freak out if she doesn't think everything looks perfect. Feeling satisfied, I hang the dress back up.

Before I can move onto the next item, my step-mother walks in and gives me the next demand. "Ella, where is breakfast?"

My step-mother's words make me flinch. Shit, I forgot to prepare breakfast before getting caught up in what Leah and Mia needed. I set all my items down and respond in a monotone voice, "I will do that now."

Jogging toward the kitchen, I hurry to make everyone their signature egg white omelets with a side of fruit. Thankfully, when it comes to food they're easy and predictable. They never eat more than what they consider the "right" amount of calories. My step-mother instilled the need to look perfect at all times into the girls. Going so far as to take food away from them, criticize them, and even tell them they weren't pretty enough. Perfect enough. Thin enough.

She tells me this too, but I just never listen. I work hard to remember my mom calling me beautiful. My dad always taking me for ice cream and calling me his perfect little girl.

I plate the food. Leave it on the counter and get ready to run the errand for Mia. I smile inwardly knowing I'm going to grab myself a coffee while I'm out. A coffee that is definitely not on the allowed to eat list and full of chocolate and whipped cream. What they don't know, won't hurt them.

And what could be bad about a little sweetness in life…right?

***

My sugar high doesn't last long. When I get back, I'm met with a stern looking step-mother sitting in an armchair in the shadows of the living room. It's obvious she has been waiting for me, probably trying to catch me doing something I'm not supposed to, so she can punish me.

"Where have you been, Ella?"

Her icy voice washes over me, turning my insides cold, but I stay steady. I pull the bag from the jeweler from behind my back and hold it up for her to see. "I went to grab the jewelry that Mia requested."

My step-mother's eyes flash quickly with anger, never leaving my face. I can tell she's pissed that I was out for Mia and not doing something nefarious, but I don't give her any sass. I don't move, nor do I flinch. I just stand there letting the silence envelop the room until she finally breaks.

She rises from the chair, and steps closer to me, not allowing me any room to move. "Fine. Finish getting the girls ready. We need to leave. And no messing around, Ella. You need to do as I say. We wouldn't want anything bad to happen to your father."

With those words, she turns to leave. My eyes close and my lungs fully inflate with air as I'm left standing there...wishing that I didn't have to deal with any of this anymore.

Climbing up the stairs, my mind drifts to my plans. Plans to go to the ball, sneak around, and hopefully find some information that makes them pay and set me free. For now, I have to stay the course so they won't see me coming. But mark my words, I will be coming for th em.

"Ella, get in here and help zip me up." Mia's words break through my thoughts. I look up at both girls dressed in matching slip dresses that mold to every curve of their body. Mia has a red dress on that compliments her dark, ebony hair while Leah is wearing a green dress that sets off the red highlights in her light brown hair. A wave of jealousy starts deep in my stomach. Shit, I don't want to be jealous of them, but these girls have always been gorgeous and it's even more glaring now that I clearly don't measure up.

The little girl in me wishes that things could be different, that I could be in a dress right now that matches them, like real sisters. That my mom and dad would be taking us to the ball. Proud. Ready to show us to the world.

I walk up behind both of them zipping up their dresses. I finish up with their makeup and hair. Giving them another glance, I can't help but let the honesty escape my mouth. "You girls look so pretty."

The soft smirk on Leah's face gives me hope that maybe we still have time to have a real relationship, but when I turn to Mia, all of those thoughts disappear as I come face to face with her wicked smile.

She looks me up and down and then flips her hair at me. With another smirk, I know I'm not going to like the next words out of her mouth.

"Yes, Ella. We do look good, don't we? We will miss you at the party, but then again no one would even know you were there, right? I know I wouldn't." The ugly step-sister. No parents. No pretty clothes. Nothing to offer anymore.

I can feel the tears start to well up in the back of my eyes. I try to blink them away before one slips. Unfortunately, I'm not fast enough, and one slides down my cheek. Using my sleeve, I try to covertly wipe it away, but Leah sees it. Her face softens a tiny bit, for just a second.

"Thank you, Ella," she whispers as she leaves me behind.

Four

Ella

Once the house is silent, I pack my purse with a few essentials. Thankfully, I don't need a dress, so sneaking out of here will be a lot easier. I head to the hall that leads to the front door as quiet as a mouse, crossing my fingers that I won't run into anyone. As soon as I step out the front door, I let out a breath I didn't even realize I was holding.

My mind swims with what could happen at the masquerade ball tonight along with all the questions that have been taking root lately. Like what is my step-mother up to? Is she really looking to find husbands for my step-sisters or are they hiding something bigger? Hopefully, tonight will bring me one step closer to the truth. Looking up, I find myself standing on the street in front of the bar. I close my eyes and pray that this is another step in securing my future, not a one way ticket to my demise.

"Hey, Amber," I call as I walk deeper into the bar.

"Back here," she yells as she looks up from whatever she's working on and gives me a soft smile. Just seeing her calms the nerves that have been floating around in my stomach.

"Come on, let's get you princess ready," she says, leading me to the locker room where the strippers get ready for their shows.

This plan still seems so crazy. I'm not convinced that no one will recognize me. Doubts start to run rampant, and my body freezes in the doorway.

"What are you doing? Stop standing there and come sit down so I can get started. You can do this. You are stronger and smarter than you think."

Shaking my head, I reply solemnly, "I'm not sure I can. I don't feel brave right now. I'm not pretty enough to be a princess. My dad was the only one ever to call me princess."

Amber leans over my shoulder, as our eyes meet in the mirror. "Ella. Don't say that. You are one of the bravest people I know and prettier than any princess. Don't let anyone ever tell you anything different. You hear me?"

I roll my eyes at her but a smirk graces my lips. "Okay, Amber. I hear you."

Her grin and easy going personality returns. When she starts to fluff my hair, she gives me a wink as she says, "Tonight you can call me your fairy godmother, Ella. But I have one condition: you can't see until I'm done, no peeking."

I return her smile, her strength and confidence seeping into my body. I place my hand on her arm. "Don't worry. I won't look. I promise. And Amber…"

"Yeah?"

"Thank you." I just barely manage to hold back my tears.

Amber gives me a wink and gets work on my hair and makeup. We talk about everything, getting to know each other even more. We talk about how the bar has turned around since she took over as manager and she tells me a little more about her childhood, and how she was taken from everything she knew.

I open up to her, telling her more about my life and how it turned upside down when my father remarried. Amber already knew about some of the things I've dealt with but she didn't know how bad it really was and still is.

The conversation keeps flowing between us like we're old friends. A warmth settles over me. I haven't felt this close to anyone since I met Suri. Suri and Amber will love each other. I should introduce them to each other. Maybe I could have some real friends and find a way for us to spend some time together.

Maybe it's wishful thinking...but it gives me something to fight for. A reason to go along with this crazy plan and try to get out from under my step-mother's thumb.

Amber brings me back to the present when she taps my shoulder. "All right, lady, let's put that beautiful dress on you. I think you're going to like it. Carly brought it just for you."

I follow her eyes to the blue sparkly gown hanging up in the corner of the room. My hand brushes against the fabric when I whisper, "It's beautiful. This is for me?"

Nodding, she helps me put the dress on, slipping on the shoes that go with it. "Are you ready to see how you look?" she asks as she looks me up and down with a twinkle in her eye.

I smooth my hands over my dress and take a deep breath. "I'm ready."

Turning to look in the mirror, all thoughts leave my brain.

"Ella, you look gorgeous!"

I can't help staring into the mirror. I run my hands lightly over my face and the ends of my hair. Fuck, is that me? No, that can't be, I've never seen myself look like this. My hair is softly curled down my back with a simple jeweled headband as if it's a tiara. My makeup is a simple natural look, with a bold red lip.

"Amber, you made me look beautiful. I look like a princess," I tell her, trying to push down the lump of emotion in my throat.

Her eyes narrow on me, "Ella, we've talked about this. I didn't make you look beautiful. You already are. Always have been inside and out," she says, leaving no room for argument.

After what feels like forever, she claps her hands together, breaking us from the spell that we seemed to be under. "Okay, enough of that mushy shit. Listen up, Paul will drop you off at the club, Midnight Blue," she says as she nods her head toward the bouncer standing by the door. "Here is your mask that you'll need for the party. I'll leave your bag here in the dressing room and you can change back into your clothes before you go home."

I nod, listening to her directions as my fingers skim the gold mask that was handed to me. Amber put so much thought into these plans.

She really is my fairy godmother.
Just call me freaking Cinderella!

Leaving the dressing room, we step in sync with each other to the entrance of the bar while Paul follows us. Outside, a black SUV idles waiting for me. I climb in and as he closes the door, I remember to yell, "Thank you, Amber."

I faintly hear her yell back, "Knock'em dead, Ella," as the car starts to roll.

I look back down at the beautiful mask. The dainty golden mask covers the top half of my face. Lace drapes over the mask giving it an elegant feel. How was she able to get such a beautiful piece so quickly? I tie the black silk ribbons around my head and send up a little prayer that no one recognizes me, especially my step-mother and step-sisters. I look out the window and watch the city as it passes me, wondering just what I'll learn tonight. What will happen to me if I get caught, and most importantly, what will happen to me if I don't?

"Ella, we're here," Paul announces.

Wow, I didn't realize I was so caught up in my own mind.

"Thank you, Paul," I say as I climb out of the car as gracefully as possible. Which is harder than you would think in a ball gown and four inch heels, but thankfully I'm able to keep my composure. I need everything to go perfectly tonight and perfect means not drawing attention to myself.

I'm literally stunned stupid when I sneak into the club. I can't seem to stop my eyes from bouncing around, not able to focus on anything specific in the room. I can't believe that my step-mother brought my step-sisters to this. What the hell am I watching? Couples, groups, singles all in various states of dress. Kissing, groping, actual goddamn sex. In the ballroom! My body slowly starts to heat up as I pass by. The deeper I go into the club, the harder it is to ignore the scenes in front of me. Part of me wants to stop and watch. The other part just wants to find the bar. I'm going to need some liquid courage for this. The blush I felt brewing seems to be consuming me now because right next to the bar…holy shit.

Right in front of me, a fit older man is sitting in a booth with a young woman on her knees in front of him. The man's hand is tangled in her hair as he directs her motions on his cock. Watching him does something to me. I can't take my eyes off them. My nipples start to pebble and I feel the wetness pool between my legs.

To the right of him, another gorgeous blonde woman takes his mouth in a searing kiss, while he is still directing the one between his knees. His other hand moves and I can't help but follow it. Those fingers start trailing up the leg of the woman kissing him until it disappears under her skirt.

My heart starts to race as the throb between my legs increases. Rubbing my thighs together, I try to alleviate it, but damn, it's not helping.

I try to reconcile what is happening in front of me with how I'm feeling. But before I can decide between embarrassed and turned on, my shoulder jolts and a gruff voice says, "Shit, I'm sorry." I look toward the voice but before I'm able to say anything the man walks off. I shake my head. I need to remember why I'm here.

I just didn't know here would be…this.

I head toward the bar. I need a drink. Maybe it will help calm down my body and then I can concentrate on why I'm here. I grab the bartender's attention.

"What can I get you?"

"A vodka soda with a lime, please."

"Coming right up."

Clearing my head from the voyeur scene, I decide I need to search the room for my step-mother and step-sisters. I look up at the balcony where the VIP section must be located. If Mia and my step-mother are here, that's where they'll be.

My eyes lock on a slightly older man leaning over the balcony, observing the club. Holy fuck...he is the most gorgeous man I have ever seen. A drink drops down in front of me and I reach for it without looking away from the sexy man. I can't see all of his face because of the black mask covering it, but his short dark brown hair is perfectly styled, except for a small piece in the front that drips down in front of his face. His strong chin covered in the perfect amount of stubble and all I want to do is rub my hands against it. He has an aura of danger that surrounds him and even with that, I can't take my eyes off him. He looks like a king surveying his kingdom.

And all I can think is...
He's mine.

Never in my life have I felt such a connection like I do when I'm looking at this man. I don't know his name. I don't know him. But I do know I feel drawn to him. Entranced. Just like you read about in fairy tales. I've never believed in that nonsense until this moment.

I run my eyes over his body, dressed in a deep navy suit. One obviously tailored specifically to fit his muscular body the way it clings to his broad shoulders and is drawn in on his tapered waist. My mouth starts to water at the thought of seeing or touching the body under that suit. I want to climb him.

What is wrong with me? I mean seriously...the thoughts I'm having are not normal.

He must feel my eyes on him because suddenly he whips his head around and looks right at me. As our eyes collide, he gives me a panty melting smile and my whole body reacts to it. I mean goosebumps all over my arms, hard nipples, and throbbing clit instantly. I thought I was turned on before, but that was nothing compared to this moment.

What is happening right now?

When the man turns to talk to someone behind him, the spell between us breaks. As reality crashes into me, a woman drapes her arm over his shoulder.

What did you think, Ella, that he was going to search you out? No, a man like that can have anyone he wants, why would he want you?

Fuck...distracted again.

I brush my hair back behind my shoulders, I'm not here for the extremely sexy stranger...I need to find out what my step-mother and step-sisters are up to. Keeping my goal in mind, I down my drink.

It's go time.

After walking away from the bar, I catch a glimpse of Mia. I follow her, staying in the shadows. She enters a room that leads to a back hallway and when she gets to the doorway at the end, I see her put in a code before going through.

I check to make sure no one is paying attention to me and make my way to the door. I try the handle but of course it's locked. What's someone trying to hide behind an encoded access only door? And why does Mia have the code?

While I'm staring at the door trying to figure out my next move, a voice comes through the speakers. I follow the sound back down the hallway and enter a room where hordes of people are sitting in chairs facing a stage.

Quickly walking around to the back of the room staying hidden in the shadows, I glance around. My step-mother is sitting close to a man that I don't recognize. He leans over as he places a hand on her thigh and whispers something in her ear. My blood starts to boil. What the hell is she doing? Cheating on my dying father? Even though I'm not entirely surprised...it hurts. My heart hurts for him even though he will most likely never know. My father is a good man and I want more for him than her.

While my mind starts to race with all possibilities of what could be happening right in front of me the light on the stage turns the audience quiet. That's when I feel it. A tingle of awareness starts to slide down my spine as the hairs on my neck stand up.

Straightening my spine and rolling my shoulders back, I stand tall keeping my attention to the stage.

Glancing over to watch my step-mother and her date, neither of them speaking, just watching as the man on the stage announces something...

Did he say an auction?

Five

Mikhail

Standing here, I soak up the energy of the room. It feels fucking amazing. The atmosphere of the club, especially on a night like tonight you can't help but get swept up. The sexual tension runs through the whole club and continues to rise with each guest that enters.

The theme tonight is masked sexual freedom. Once a month, I host a party just like tonight. Guests are required to wear a mask to hide their identity, allowing powerful players to enjoy anonymously. It offers the freedom of indulgence without any real consequence. For added protection, we do make participants sign an NDA, get searched upon entering, and the club is littered with recording devices.

It keeps our clients safe from each other but not from me. Tonight, I will be collecting their preferences and deeds as insurance policies. Insurance against my enemies. Insurance against my friends. I trust no one. Leaning over the balcony, I watch. Some guests stare and gawk, some look on with longing and interest, while others engage in sexual activities. You can taste the excitement in the air.

At a table below me is the mayor and his wife. As regulars at these parties, they really enjoy themselves.

I watch as he spreads his wife out over the table. From this position, I can't see her pussy– only the sly look on her face that tells me she's loving what he's doing to her. Closing her eyes, she throws her head back as he eats her pussy like a starving man.

I can't help but smirk. I love to watch and these two love to be watched.

The room is dark, but I can just imagine her juices dripping down his face. When she comes hard, he looks up at me and winks.
Fucking winks.

I adjust my hardening cock as I continue to watch. No one ever joins in the fun...our illustrious mayor doesn't share. In the recesses of my mind, I reluctantly acknowledge that the idea of having someone who belongs only to me could be something that I might want in the future. When it comes to relationships, I keep them as simple as possible. I don't do repeats. I don't do feelings. I don't do attachments. I keep things as clean as possible. It's easier, especially with the life

I lead. Women don't understand my lifestyle and I haven't found anyone I want to explain things to.

I tip my chin at the mayor and continue to admire this small piece of heaven that I've built. I can't help but preen a little knowing that I was able to accomplish this without anyone's help. Especially not my father's.

My father, the Pakhan of the Russian Bratva. He loves to be in control and that includes my life. I was able to keep this club out of his hands as long as I continue to do my duty as his heir.

I touch the solid black mask on my face that resembles the phantom, ensuring it's still in place. Everyone here knows who I am but I like to keep up appearances for the parties' sake.

Suddenly, I freeze. In my thirty-four years, I have never seen a more beautiful woman. She's standing at the bar with light shining behind her, illuminating her like an angel from heaven.

My angel put on this earth for me...just me.

The woman is wearing a pale blue strapless dress that sparkles under the lights of the club giving her an even more ethereal feel. The material clings to every curve. And for fucks sake...she's got curves. I can tell she's younger than me, but I don't give a shit about that. Her dark, chestnut brown hair curls down her back and I want to wrap it around my hand and tilt her head back as her luscious lips wrap around my cock.

When she looks up and our eyes meet, my cock hardens against the front of my jeans. Fuck! I thought she was beautiful before, but her light blue eyes hypnotize me even more. What is happening to me? I have never been instantly drawn to a woman like this before.

As we stare into each other's eyes, I can't help but wonder what she's thinking. Is she wondering what my rough hands will feel like roaming over her body as I worship her? Or maybe what it might be like down on her knees as she takes me all the way down her throat?

Her mask leaves only her eyes, and pouty lips exposed. The Rolodex of invited guests plays through my mind, but I can't place her. Who is she?

"Mr. Sokolov…"

My body wants her…I need to touch her…have her…at least for tonight. *Maybe forever…*

"Mr. Sokolov…can I get you anything?"

I turn toward the high-pitched feminine voice, and I can't help but frown. Standing in front of me is one of the club's waitresses, Anya. She has her hand on her hips, pushing out her lips, while she waits for my answer. What was it she wanted? I furrow my brows. "What did you say, Anya? I didn't hear you."

She flutters her eyelashes at me. "Mr. Sokolov…do you need me to get you anything?"

She enunciates each word making sure that I understand she's asking for more than my drink order. Anya is a beautiful woman. Any man would be happy to be with her, but not me. Not tonight. In the past we've played together, but now watching her my cock doesn't even stir. Not like it did when I saw the princess in the blue dress. "I'm good, Anya."

"Are you sure?" she says as she walks towards me. Then she drapes her arms around my neck and whispers, "I can make you feel really good."

Not wanting to engage in this with her, I gently remove her hands from me and answer, "I'm good. I don't need anything or want anything tonight, Anya."

I stare at her, my body language and harsh tones letting her know I mean business as I take a step to the side to put distance between us.

She doesn't take the hint.

Fluttering her lashes, she continues to stick out her lips in a pout. "Oh come on, Mikhail, you don't have to be like that. I just wanted to have some fun."

"It's Mr. Sokolov, Anya. I need you to listen to me and listen good. We're done. We will never happen again so forget any time we've ever spent together in the past. And you would do well to remember what happens if you can't follow my rules."

I only want the dark-haired beauty downstairs.

I glance back at the bar to look for the woman again but go rigid when I realize she's gone. Shit. Anya distracted me and now I don't know where she is or if she left. Time to go find her.

"Excuse me, Anya," I say as I push past her and head downstairs to see if I can find my woman. *Wait, what? When did she become my woman?*

I slowly walk through the swarm of people, kissing, making out, and fucking. Fuck…I might find her participating in a scene and honestly I might lose it if I do. I don't know how, but in one glance I claimed this woman. I may not know her name, but I know she belongs to me.

I just fucking hope she feels the same way.

As I turn the corner, I spot a blur of blue dress and dark hair going down a hall that leads to another room.

"Shit," I mumble to myself. She's heading to a place that I'm not sure she wants to find herself in: the auction room. Where single guests put themselves up for sale to find a sex partner for the night.

I need to get to her. I can't let that happen. If she is going to be with anyone tonight, it's going to be with me. I take off, almost running through the club. The crowd is thick at the entrance of the room as guests pile into the room to find a seat. I lose sight of her. Where could she have gone? Scanning the room, I let out a breath when I spot her, and she hasn't seemed to have drawn anyone else's attention.

She stands in the shadows looking toward the stage. I don't want to spook her, so I stop. Wait. Simply observe her as she watches with wide eyes, her brain trying to take in what she's seeing. I slink toward her as quietly as possible making sure that she doesn't see me.

I slide up behind her just close enough for her to feel the heat of my body. I know the moment she feels me because her fingers start to twitch. She doesn't turn, doesn't make a sound. If it wasn't for a few small tells, I would think that she didn't know I was there. I lean in, allowing my breath to skitter over her neck. "Hello, baby girl."

Her pulse picks up as she engages with me. She looks nervous and ready to bolt for a second before she finds her resolve. Pulling back her shoulders, she stands tall and turns her head and looks right at me. It feels like she looks right into me. Like she can read everything about me. The blood rushes to my head and then straight to my cock. All the sounds of the room fade away until all I can see is her. She looks younger than I thought and even more beautiful up close. Before words even leave my mouth, she says quietly "I'm not here for you." Turning her body back toward the auction, she ignores me. She fucking ignores me. No, that won't do.

My mind starts to race, and I can't help but wonder why she came to this room specifically.

"Do you know what this room is, baby girl?"

Her lips twitch trying not to smile at my words. She shakes her head at me. "It doesn't matter. I'm here for one thing and one thing only."

Moving her hair out of the way, I whisper. "And what is that for?"

Her neck starts to turn red and her eyes start to get wide as she looks past my shoulder. "It's not your concern," she says and walks away. Chasing whatever caught her attention.

Baby girl...everything about you is my concern, you just don't know it yet.

I follow her back into the main room and find her standing in the center looking confused as she searches the room. Her eyes have a sad determination to them that I'm not fucking okay with. If some bastard made her sad, he's going to pay. I need to know what or who she's searching for. And why.

When I reach her, I grab her arm, spinning her to look at me. She looks surprised. "You followed me."
"Always."

The look she gives me makes my cock even harder than earlier.

"Fuck, I want to kiss you, baby girl."

"You don't even know my name," she whispers back.

I wrap my hands around her waist pulling her into me, "Tell me then, baby girl. What's your name?"

She hesitates worrying that bottom lip between her teeth before saying, "No. Let's keep it simple. I need it simple."

Before I can argue, she wraps her arms around my neck, pulls me down to her level and kisses me. Her mouth parts and I can't help but take advantage of it. I press my tongue into her mouth and taste her for the first time. She tastes like vodka, lime, and a hint of strawberries. Fucking heaven. I wrap my arms around her waist and pull her against me, hard. I want her to know what she does to me.

When she pulls away from me, I can't help but smile at her puffy lips. "Ok, baby girl, we can do it your way. For now."

Leaning down, I snuggle into her hair, rubbing my nose along the column of her neck. Basking in her beauty. Wanting to get lost in her. "You look so beautiful, all perfectly kissed," I say as I run my thumb along her bottom lip. "Why don't we go find somewhere to be alone?"

"I'm not sure that's a good idea," she says as she shakes her head, and I can tell that she's getting ready to flee.

I tighten my hold on her, probably leaving bruises on her hips but I need her close. "Baby girl, this isn't a night for thinking, this is a night for feeling."

She doesn't say any words, but her eyes never leave mine as I press my cock against her belly, making sure she feels what she's doing to me. Her lids become hooded, her cheeks blush and I hear her sharp intake of breath.

I see it happen. When she accepts the inevitable and gives me the green light. I step back with my hand wrapped around hers and I pull her urgently through the club.

Deep inside a flicker of insecurity sparks, making me feel like if I need to hurry up and convince her I'm hers or I could possibly lose her. Like I lost my mom. In the Bratva, everyone is scheming and always wants something from you, especially when you are the son of the Pakhan. Including women. My mom was the only one I could depend on when I was younger. I thought she would be around forever. But fate had other ideas, taking my mom away from me at seventeen. A hit and run. It took only one minute and she was gone.

My father has never recovered. She was the love of his life. He has always wanted this for me and to continue our family line for the Bratva. I saw what the accident did and how it destroyed him, which is why I've never had a serious relationship. But now I can't stop thinking about making this woman mine.

We make our way through the maze of people, climbing the stairs toward the second level of the club, and down a quiet hallway to my office. Swinging open the door, she looks around the room and lets out a small gasp. "You work here?"

Pulling her into my office, I close the door behind her, and drop down on the couch in the corner of my office with her on my lap. "I don't just work here. I own the club," I say as I tilt my head back toward her and rub my tongue across her lips, wanting access to her mouth. She lets me in and hums with satisfaction.

Fuck, I'm in trouble.

Six

Ella

I want to ask him so many questions, especially about tonight and the club but something stops me. Keeping my mouth shut, I let him lick across my lips, causing me to hum in appreciation.

This time though, I need him. Between him and everything I saw earlier, I'm feeling desperate.

"More," I all but moan.

The sexy man doesn't even waste a moment; he slides me off his lap. Placing me next to him as he lifts his body to hover over me, pushing me down on the couch. He looks down at me, "Shit, baby girl, you are something else."

His hands trail down my body as if he's memorizing it.

"I bet you are wet for me, baby. Show me."

I don't say anything. I've never been one to speak much in the bedroom, but I do exactly as he asked. Pulling my dress up over my hips, I spread my legs wide giving him better access to my pussy. He leans down and drags his fingers over my underwear.

"Fucking hell."

Sliding his hands up my thighs, he places his thumbs on the waistband of my panties and pulls them slowly down my legs. Painfully slow. Once they are off, he brings them to his face and smells them. I can feel the blush creep up my neck watching him.

"Fuck, woman, you are my favorite smell now."

Before I can even let out a breath, he dives into my pussy licking me all the way down my slit. And, hell yes, it feels amazing. "Oh God…"

Swirling the tip of his tongue at the edges of my clit feels amazing. I tighten my hands in the fabric of my dress, needing something to grasp. Something to ground me in the moment.

How does this man, who I don't even really know, play my body like it's an instrument that only he was meant to play? I feel the tingle and the heat from my core start to rise.

"Please…" I moan.

"Please what, baby girl?"

I don't answer. I grab his head, tangling my hands in his hair to keep him place. He sucks me harder, and fuck, I shout, "I'm coming."

I grind my hips against his face as he softly licks me through my orgasm. When my breathing settles, he grins at me. I smile back at him and then flop my head back on the couch, closing my eyes. "I-I don't even know what to say. I don't usually do this kind of thing. Maybe I should just...go."

That's when I hear him chuckle and then his deep timber voice say, "Baby girl, I'm not nearly done with you."

Seven

Mikhail

She's so fucking cute...all nervous and antsy. But she's not leaving. And if I have it my way, she will never leave.

So I lean back on the couch and pull her up, grabbing her legs and placing them on either side of mine so that she straddles me. I can feel the heat from her pussy through my pants and my dick, which was already hard, takes notice. I push her dark hair off her shoulders exposing her collar bone. My fingers draw down into the valley of her breasts, as I pull down her dress to expose her tits, but it resists. I let out a huff, trying to pull harder. She lets out a giggle and reaches over to her side unzipping the dress. The front of it falls and leaves me with the most perfect set of tits I've ever seen.

MIDNIGHT BLUE 51

Her pink nipples are pointing right at me. I lean down and suck them into my mouth. She arches her back and starts grinding on me even more. I wrap my arms around her back, sliding them up and down her spine.

"That's it, baby girl, grind on daddy, just like that."

Daddy?

I've never had a woman call me daddy before, but it feels right. Maybe because she's young or it could be because I have this innate feeling to protect her.

My cock is hard and throbbing, but I want to feel all of her. Her mouth. Her pussy. Her ass.

Reading my mind, she slips her delicious nipple from my mouth and slides down my body. When she hits her knees, her hands reach out and start to unbuckle my belt. She slowly slides my zipper down until my thick cock springs out. Her eyes never leave my dick and when her tongue darts out to lick her lips, I nearly come.

The look in her eyes, her quick shallow breaths, and the scent of her arousal turns me on in a way I've never felt. Before taking me into her mouth, she looks up.

"Take off your dress, baby girl. I want to see all of you."

"You first," she whispers.

I unbutton my tuxedo shirt and slide it down my arms, her eyes follow my every move, and her reaction is everything. She stares at me like I'm a work of art. And damn does that inflate my ego just a bit. When she draws her finger across the muscles on my abdomen, I clench. She looks up at me and murmurs, "You are so beautiful."

Her eyes go wide and her cheeks flood with embarrassment. I'm guessing she didn't mean to say that out loud. Hoping to erase those feelings, I give her a soft kiss, "Not as beautiful as you."

Ready to feel her mouth on my cock, I tug my pants off as she leans back on her heels watching me the whole time, her eyes hooded with lust. "Now it's your turn, baby girl. I want to see all of you too."

She stands up quickly, ridding herself of her dress. She's stunning. With her dress gone she drops back to her knees and wraps her small hands around my cock. I let out a hiss of pleasure and take a deep breath, not wanting this to be over before it even starts.

Giving me a smirk, knowing what she's doing to me, she slides my whole cock into her mouth, rubbing me against her tongue. Instinctively, my hands go to her hair. I just hold her, not pushing. I want her to do what feels good to her, but fuck... her mouth. She takes me so deep she gags a little and pulls back. "That's right, baby girl, take my cock. You're such a good girl."

She starts to swirl her tongue around the head of my cock, and I feel my cock thicken but I'm not ready to come yet, so I pull her off. "Daddy loved that baby girl, but I need to be inside you."

Grabbing under her arms, I pull her up commanding, "Straddle me."

She plants her knees on either side of me lining up my cock with her dripping pussy. I thrust up into her and she glides her fingers through my hair on the back of my head. We start moving in unison, skin slapping against each other. I can feel her dripping down onto my balls and it takes every ounce of my control not to come. She moans again, "Harder, Daddy."

Well, fuck. Calling me daddy is like a bolt of pleasure to my cock. Damn, that's hot. I need her to come *now*, so I press my fingers to her clit. "Come with me, baby girl. Come for daddy."

"Fuck...Daddy...I'm coming."

With those words, her pussy chokes my cock, milking me in rhythmic waves. My balls draw up, my eyes close and for the first time ever I see stars. I let go, painting the insides of her walls with my cum.

Leaning my head against her forehead, both of our eyes closed, all you can hear is heartbeats and panting. "Shit, baby girl, I don't think I've ever come so hard."

She lets out a scoff and then smiles at me. "I don't usually orgasm like that either."

"Well, just give me a few minutes and then we can go again." Sucking my fingers in my mouth, I trail them down her ass finding her forbidden hole inserting one finger saying, "But next time, I'll be taking that ass."

I scissor my fingers, stretching her, to get her ready for our next round. I lean down and kiss the tip of her nose.

And right then, I know I won't let her go. I need to know everything about her. Not just what her body likes but what her heart, mind and soul need too. Before all of this is done, she will be mine.

Eight

Mikhail

Awareness starts to trickle in. I haven't slept that well in a long time. The memories of the night before come flooding back to me, and fuck, it was a good night. I ended up taking her two more times and I did indeed have all of her like I wanted. Once we exhausted ourselves we passed out on the couch in my office.

The thought of the dark-haired beauty I spent the night with has me wanting to feel her up against me again. The heat from her body isn't pressed against me. Where could she be? I open up my eyes and glance around the office. I don't see her. How did she sneak out without me hearing? Sitting straight up, I still don't see her so I get up to check the hallway. But I know deep down that she isn't here anymore.

I didn't even make her give me her name. Fuck I knew agreeing to not revealing who we were was a bad idea. I'd assumed I would have time to convince her to give me her name and to never leave my side before she left. Obviously, she thought differently.

I pull out my phone to call Sergei, because I need him to track her down. We must have security footage of her. And she was here at an invite only party, so someone must know who she is. I will find her. Even if I have to go door to door in the whole fucking city. I won't give up until she is back in my arms.

I search the office. Maybe she left something behind, that will give me a clue of who she could be. Something catches my attention, glinting in the sun in the corner of the room. Bingo, this should help me find her.

And once I get her back, she will never leave me again. I'll give her everything. My name. My home. My protection. My…love. I graze my finger across the golden mask that she was wearing. It's so delicate but strong just like the woman that wore it.

Dialing Sergei, he answers, "Boss."

"I need you to find someone for me."

He chuckles at my request like he knows something I don't. "Is it the little lady you were with last night?"

"Don't fucking start. But yes. We didn't exchange names, but she left her mask behind. I'll send you a picture, so you can find her on surveillance. I want to know everything about her, right down to her shoe size."

"Got it, boss."

"And Sergei?"

"Yes?"

"Let's keep this between us for right now."

And with those words I hang up on him. He's my right-hand man for a reason and is loyal as they come. He's been with me since I was a kid, his dad one of my father's soldiers. I can't risk anyone knowing about her or our connection until I can make sure I keep her safe. My club might be a legit business, what happens below isn't. That's where I gather the information, I need by any means necessary, for the Bratva, for my father. And since I'm so good at my job, I've created enemies too.

I can't help but think of what the future with her could be like. Things that I've never thought about before. I see her in a white dress walking down the aisle to me, swollen with my child, and I know deep down that there is no way that I would be able to leave her behind. She was made for me.

My phone buzzes, interrupting my thoughts. Glancing down, Zeev's name on the screen forces my body to stiffen up. Transitioning into business mode, I reply quickly, agreeing to the meet up.

The Bratva are a part of a group of leaders from different mafias. We get together to discuss matters, making sure we keep the peace in the area. Zeev and his wife became the leaders of Le Milieu, the French Mafia, after taking down the previous leader, her grandmother. Even though they are both in charge, he tends to deal with the darker matters.

I send an address off to Zeev for the meet. I chose a bar that is in between our two territories. My client Max from the club owns it, and he has offered it as a place to conduct business.

Throwing on my clothes from last night, I head out to my apartment. I need to freshen up and eat. I just hope that Sergei is able to get the information on my mystery woman. And soon.

***

I park my Lamborghini in front of a nondescript building with a sign that reads, The Tower. This is it. Turning off the car, I head inside. I made sure to show up a little bit early. I've never been here before. I wanted to check it out before Zeev arrived.

Inside the bar, the atmosphere is calm with only a few other patrons, two of them sitting at the bar and two other groups stationed at tables on opposite sides of the bar. It's just your run of the mill location full of "normal" people. This is perfect.

I head toward the back where a blonde woman behind the bar looks up at me, giving me a friendly greeting, "Welcome. Feel free to find a seat anywhere and I'll be over to grab your drink order."

I nod my head in thanks, taking a seat at a booth in the back of the room. With a view of the whole bar, and no one around us, I'm confident we'll be able to meet in private. It will be easy to know if someone tries to sneak up on us while we are talking. Zeev and Jake, his right-hand man, walk in and sit down.

"Hey, guys."

"Mikhail. We've found some information for you," Zeev says, getting right to the point. That's what I like about him, he's not one to pussy foot around.

I nod, "Brian has intel that we all could have possible rats in our organizations, and they are the ones who are stealing weapons."

Brian is the head of the Irish Mafia. Furrowing my brow, I take in this new information. I need to smoke out whoever could be giving away our secrets. We don't do rats.

"Do we know who they're working for?"

"Not yet."

Pulling out my phone, I start to make note of all the things that I need to do to make sure this situation doesn't get more out of hand. I pull up Sergei's contact so that he can help look into all of this. But before I can call him, a feminine voice interrupts, "Sorry to bother you but what can I...." Her voice trails off.

I look up and see her and Jake locked in an intense stare, neither of them saying a word. Zeev clears his throat, seeming to break whatever the hell was going on between them. She shakes her head. "I'm sorry...I can't..." Running off before she even finishes her thought.

"Shit, I can't believe it," Jake says but I don't think he's talking to us.

"Jake, what was that?" I ask. But he doesn't answer me, just gets up and goes after the woman without saying a word.

Across the table, Zeev looks just as confused as I feel.

"What do you think that was about?"

"I don't know, but I've never seen Jake chase after a woman before."

Needing to get the meeting back on track I return to the situation at hand. "Okay, well. I will talk to my father and our contacts to see what else we can find out about the rats."

Tapping my knuckles on the table, I stand up and leave The Tower behind. Fuck, now I really do need to find the mystery woman from last night before anyone else does.

Nine

Ella

Waking up this morning, I'm still not sure how to feel about everything that went down last night, other than the fact that I had the best sex of my life. But I am still in shock about finding my step-mother at some auction, seeing Mia go behind closed doors to do god knows what, and I never even saw Leah.

I thought going to the party last night would give me answers. Instead, I just walked away with more questions. If I want to know more about what is happening, I'm going to have to look for the answers myself.

With a feeling of determination, I pop out of bed and get ready for the day. I put on my black leggings and tank top to ensure I'm comfortable while snooping in the house. One good thing about growing up in this old house, I know all the hidden passageways. Making it easy to get around without being seen.

I head downstairs to the kitchen to see if anyone is home. If anyone is here, they will come down to grab breakfast. The house is really quiet, and no one is moving around which just confirms my suspicions that none of them came home last night.

I pull out the ingredients to make myself an omelet. If anything, I'll get to eat in peace *and* eat what I want. Placing my phone next to me on the counter, I turn on my Spotify playlist and start cooking. The music allows me to forget everything. When I'm moving my body to the beat, I forget that my father is sick and, in the hospital, that the step-witches are up to something and that I've never felt anything like I did last night with any man before.

My mind drifts to the mystery man and how it felt when his rough hands ran all over my body, touched my nipples, and played my clit like an instrument. He even took my ass in one of our rounds, something I've never done before. But I ran. I snuck out in the middle of the night and now the sadness is trying to take me down, but I can't let it.

Since no one has made an appearance, I finish eating and muster the courage to try and find the answers I need. Going up the back staircase hidden in the kitchen, I arrive directly to the wing where my step-sisters have their rooms.

Weighing the pros and cons, I decide to search Mia's room first. Hers seems to be safer than my step-mom's room, Leah's room, or the office. If I get caught, I'll just pretend to be cleaning something.

Looking around, I try to figure out where I should start. I pull out her nightstand drawers but quickly close them because they only contain old pictures from high school and some sex toys which I didn't need to know that she had.

I check out the closet next. If it was me, that's where I would hide something of value. I rake through the clothes to see if she has any hidden boxes behind them. Glancing up at the shelves, I notice a lone black box–

Stepping on my tip toes, I reach for it and grab it with my fingertips. When I open it, I get more confused than ever. There are pictures of her with much older men in compromising positions. Underneath the pictures, I find a ledger with names, dates, how much they paid, and who fulfilled the order.

Oh. My. God. My step-mother is auctioning off her own daughters for their bodies and then taking pictures of them for blackmail. My face twists in disgust. I can't believe this is what they're up to. That's when a lightbulb goes off, fuck, this is how she has so much money, when I don't have any.

But why would Mia have the ledger and not my step-mother. Glancing back through the pictures, I see that some of them actually have my step-mother in them and others have Mia but none of them seem to have Leah in them. Maybe Mia and I aren't that much different. Maybe she is cruel to me because we are the same. Both of us are just trying to get away from the one who wants to keep us all under her thumb.

A loud noise comes from downstairs "Shit," I mumble. Sweat starts to trickle down my spine as I hurry to shove everything back in the box. Placing it back on the shelf, I try to quietly get out of the closet.

The sound of the shoes on the stairs causes my pulse to pick up. I desperately scan the room looking for something to clean. A pile of dirty clothes. Yes!

As the footsteps come closer, I quickly move across the room, keeping my back to the door and trying to act as nonchalantly as possible. Gathering the clothes, I hear Mia's screechy voice, "What are you doing in here?"

I slowly turn toward her trying not to give my thoughts away, keeping my voice calm. "I'm getting the laundry."

Turning my focus back to the dirty clothes, I continue to gather them and ignore Mia, trying to keep my hands from shaking. I don't need Mia to be suspicious. I need her to think that I'm just doing my regular chores. I don't look at her, because if I do, I might give myself away. Once I've gathered all the clothes in my hands, I go to leave the room as fast as possible.

Ten

Ella

Returning to work is harder than I thought. It's still hard to believe that I spent the night living a fairy tale just thirty six hours ago and now I'm back in the nightmare of my life. Killing myself doing chores at the house, walking on eggshells then going to work all night at the bar.

At least when I'm at The Tower, I'm finally able to relax. Or at least relax more than I can when I'm at home surrounded by my wretched family, for lack of a better word. This place sometimes feels more like home than my real home, and the people here are more of my family than those who are legally.

I shove my purse into my locker and check my phone one last time. I only see messages from Suri. I haven't responded yet and the guilt of avoiding her is starting to eat at me. I vow right then that the next time I'm off, I'm going to have to make time to see her. I miss her. I know she's been dealing with a lot, with Brendan and her family's hot and cold behavior.

For some reason when I don't see any other messages, I feel disappointed. Which is ridiculous since I didn't even give the man my number. When I really reflect on it though, I think I'm more disappointed in myself because instead of being brave and telling him my name, I took the cowardly way out. Now I'm ruined. I'll never experience anything like that again. I'll end up measuring every future lover against him, and I already know no one will ever come close.

I put my phone back in my locker to prevent me from dwelling on my mistake and spending my shift checking for messages. I'm ready to get lost in more mundane activities. Over the years I've learned that sometimes peace comes in the form of routine, and doing things that are normal. When I need normalcy in life, I clean, organize, and stick to a schedule.

I quickly look around for Amber. I can't wait to tell her about my night. It's weird that she hasn't called to ask me about it, but I know she's busy.

When I take my place behind the bar, Amber is nowhere around. *Hmm...that's weird. She's always at the bar.*

A customer gets my attention, so I walk over distractedly, "What can I get you?"

"Whiskey. Neat."

For the next hour, it's just a constant making of drinks and listening to customers ramble on and on about their lives.

When the bar calms down and I still haven't seen Amber, I start to get a little worried. She usually loves to mingle with the customers. That's what makes her a great manager.

I see Paul standing by the door. If anyone knows where she could be, it will be him. As a bouncer at the bar, he looks like a big scary guy but I know he's actually a teddy bear, especially toward Amber.

"Hey, Paul," I call.

Returning my smile, he looks over at me, "Hey, Ella. How are you tonight?"

Shrugging my shoulders because even though I like Paul I'm not going to dive into what I've been dealing with lately. "I'm good."

Paul gives me a look like I'm full of shit but he keeps his mouth shut and just dips his head in acknowledgement and goes back to counting customers. "Paul, do you know where Amber is? I haven't seen her at the bar yet."

He stares right in my eyes like he is trying to assess my intentions. I wonder what happened in the last couple of days that made him so wary. "She's in her office. Ella... she could use a girlfriend."

Softening my eyes, I place my hand on his forearm replying, "I'll go check on her then. Thanks."

He doesn't say anything else, just returns to his job. I head toward the office, and softly rap on the door. A soft voice answers me, "Come in."

When I open the door, I come face to face with Amber. Her eyes are rimmed with redness and she's obviously been crying. I close the space between us and do the only thing I know to do. I wrap my arms around her shoulders and tightly hug her. Suri always gives me a hug when everything just becomes too much, and it always helps me. I'm hoping that I can do the same for Amber.

When I first embrace her, her body goes stiff like she isn't sure what to do, but after a few minutes, she relaxes. I let go and step back, gently asking her, "What's going on, Amber?"

Sniffling, she wipes her eyes and nose with the back of her hand as she answers. "Someone from my past has shown up."

"Who?" I immediately ask, and then cringe. I need to be more careful and not push.

I don't know the whole story, but I know enough about her past to know this must be a lot for her.

"Do you want to talk about it? You don't have to if you don't want to?"

With my words, I watch her eyes harden and her walls go back up. But it doesn't bother me, we all have things that we guard harder than others. Waving me off, she answers, "No."

"Well, I'm here if you need me. Anytime."

Her face softens a tiny bit. "Thank you, Ella. Maybe someday. But enough about me, tell me what happened at the party."

I tell her all about what I saw at the party. Mia going behind the weird locked door, the auction, my step-mother sitting with a strange man, and then the pictures that I found in Mia's room when I was snooping.

"That's a lot, Ella. I'm not even sure how to process all of that? But if you need any help, you let me know," she demands.

After giving me her orders, she grins. "Did you at least get to have some fun?"

Smiling so big that my cheeks start to hurt, I tell her, "Yes. I met the sexiest man alive."

Then I tell her everything about my night with the mystery man. For once, I allow myself to bask in my new friendship and have girl talk. For the first time in a long time, I allow myself to hope that one day I will be free and able to live life like a normal twenty-four year old woman. But that's the thing about hope, it can be easily squashed by the likes of reality.

Eleven

Mikhail

In the basement of my club, I stand in front of a man I'd considered a friend but have come to find out is a traitor. I interrogated him this week and discovered he's the leak. After the tip from Zeev, my sole focus became finding the rat or rats as quickly as possible. Every organization apparently has a rat supplying information to another mafia. Somehow, these rats thought they could infiltrate the Bratva and get away with it. Well, now everyone will know that no one gets away with betraying us.

Squeezing my hands by my side, I look down at the pathetic man sitting in front of me. And I snarl. This fucker thought he could get away with it. Grabbing his sweat and blood soaked hair, I pull back his head so I can look him straight in the eyes. "How could you, Ivan? What did they offer you?"

He struggles with me, trying to get me to release my hands from his hair, but I tighten my hold. Blood drips down his face, his eyes swollen from where I'd already punched him. His cheek is swelling and turning purple already. "Pppplease, Mikhail. They threatened my family," he stutters out between harsh breaths.

"I don't care," I roar. "You should've trusted in the Bratva. We would have protected you and your family."

I pull my arm back and punch him in the face again, releasing his hair as his head snaps back. I lean down, sneering at him. "But they offered you money too, right Ivan? You couldn't help yourself, could you? You are fucking pathetic."

"Sergei, knife." I hold my hand out, and without question, he puts it in my hand.

I keep my eyes on Ivan, pop it open, then kneel down so that I'm eye level with him. Men like him feel invincible, but when he sees the look on my face, the fear sets in. That just might get him to release all the information that he knows.

"Now, Ivan, we know you're the rat, but I need you to tell me the names of the others and who you work for." Patting his cheek, I whisper, "We both know that you aren't leaving this room, Ivan, but what you tell me will decide if you die as a traitor or as a friend. Fast or slow...you choose."

He looks at me long and hard, probably trying to figure out what his best plan of action. I don't really care what he chooses. Either way, he dies and he dies at my hand. I just need the information and the more the better.

"Time is ticking, Ivan. Don't make me choose for you," I say as I rub my knife against his cheek.

This is where I feel like my true self, unleashing the violence that always strums underneath my skin. The only time I've ever felt calm was when I was with my baby girl the other night. Tired of waiting, I stab Ivan in the hand. "Ivan, tell me who you're working for?" I scream.

"A group within the G...German mafia," he answers.

"A name, Ivan. Who approached you?"

He shakes his head. "I...I don't know. A woman."

Not wanting to draw this out even more I grab my gun from the back of my waistband and shoot him right between his eyes. Tucking my gun back where it belongs, I move to the counter and grab the towel sitting there, wiping the blood off my hands and face. "Sergei, any news?"

"I only have a name, sir. Ella Thomas. But I'm still looking for her."

Goddammit, why is this taking so long? Throwing the towel down, I turn to Sergei and soak him in my anger. "I'm the fucking son of the

Pakhan, I have more money than god. Why is it that we can't find one measly woman?"

"Sir, I have my best guy looking for her."

"Not good enough, Sergei. I thought you could handle this. Was I wrong?"

He flinches a little and I know that my comment hit the mark. One of his weaknesses is that he doesn't like to feel like he's failing me.

"Sorry, sir. We will find her. I will increase the number of men looking for her."

I don't say anything else. Pulling out my phone, I call my father to inform him of what we found out.

He answers on the first ring. "Son."

"Pakhan, Ivan was the rat. He says it was the German Mafia that approached him."

I don't add anything else. No small talk, just the facts. My father doesn't do small talk, everything is about the Bratva, especially since my mom died.

He stays silent for a long moment then he clears his throat. "You are sure, Mikhail?"

"Yes, he confessed. I will let the others know and see what else I can find out about the German Mafia from our contacts."

Coughing, he clears his throat. "Yes. You do that."

Then the phone goes dead. I briskly leave the basement of the club without saying a word. Sergei knows how this works. He will contact the cleaners and continue to work on finding Ella for me. Making my way through the empty club, I jog up the stairs to the second floor where my sanctuary lies, my office.

I head to the closet and grab the first suit I can get my hands on. I need to get out of these clothes. I don't want that fucker's blood splattered all over my shirt. I take it off, I look at it, and toss it in the trash.

Then I send a text to Zeev updating him on the information that we learned from Ivan. I look at the clock and I'm thankful that it's almost time to open. Cause I need a damn drink and to lose myself in the energy that the club always brings. For now, I will try to get some of this paperwork done.

***

Hearing the strum of music through the walls has me realizing that the club is open. I must've gotten lost in the club's paperwork more than I thought. I was just trying to pass the time, so that I don't go crazy. Deciding to put it all away and head down to the club, I take the stairs two at a time and stand at the bottom of them. I take a deep breath, taking in the smell of the club. The sweat, the alcohol, and the scent of lust fills my lungs. I love it.

That's when I see it, a blur of dark chestnut hair. Could it be that easy? Is that my mystery woman? From here it's hard to see if it really is her, but I can't pull my eyes away just in case. As I continue to look out at the dance floor, one of my bodyguards taps me on the shoulder, whispering in my ear, "You have company. Looks to be the O'Sullivan boys."

I turn and what do you know? It is the O'Sullivan boys. I grin at them. "Boys, so happy you're here."

Brendan, the younger one, puts his hand out for me to shake. I return it while he speaks. "Mikhail, it's been a bit. I love what you've done to the place."

Kieran agrees, "Yes, this is something." But as he says it I can tell he's not fully paying attention to our conversation. He seems to be somewhere else as he stares across the room.

Brendan doesn't mix words as he jumps right into business. "I heard that you might have gotten some information that you wanted to share with us."

"Yes, the rat we found said that a group of rebels within the German Mafia are the ones who have been stealing weapons from us. It seems a woman is involved somehow. That's it. I guess they are not as stable as they like everyone to think they are."

"Do you have any thoughts of who it could be?" Brendan asks.

I think about his question before answering, Ivan only mentioned a woman, but I can let him know who I've encountered within the German Mafia. "No. I've had some run-ins with a Johann, but that doesn't answer why he would be stealing weapons from Zeev and you."

Brendan seems to contemplate my answer when he starts to speak. "Not sure who this Johann could be. I've never heard of him but maybe Da had some run-ins with him..."

He stops mid-sentence when he zones in on someone. I follow his gaze and shit, that's my mystery woman, Ella. She's dancing with another young woman and Brendan better keep his eyes on her or we're going to have some issues. I grit my teeth wondering how or if he might know her.

But when another man saddles up behind the other young woman, he stiffens and spits out, "Motherfucker."

Thank fuck.

I follow him because it's time for me to introduce myself and get what I want.

Ella Thomas.

Twelve

Ella

Tonight is my first night off in a while and the guilt I've been feeling about not making time for Suri has started to get to me more and more. She is one of the only people that is a constant light in my life. I really need to start doing better. An idea starts to form in my mind. Midnight Blue just opened up for regular club hours. Maybe I'll see if she wants to check it out with me. And maybe the sexy owner might be there too? A girl can only hope.

Grabbing my phone off the nightstand, I message Suri.

> **Me:** Hey want to check out a new club tonight?

While I wait for Suri to answer, I switch to my Instagram app and scroll through my feed. I don't usually post on it but I'm friends with a ton of people that I went to high school with. I stop on a profile, but the account isn't what catches my attention. It's the picture itself. Mia is in the background talking to an older gentleman. They're leaning into each other like lovers, but her eyes say something different. I'm zooming in trying to decipher what I'm seeing when Suri's response pops up.

Suri: Yes! Let's do it.

I'll have to do more digging online about Mia some other time.

I respond to her immediately, asking her to meet me at the club around nine o'clock. I have a few hours to get ready and I can't think of anything I can wear that I want to be seen in, especially if I see him.

Grabbing my keys and wallet, I head out to go shopping. Walking up to a small boutique a few blocks away from the house, the excitement from earlier flares. Not only am I determined to have fun tonight, I also made enough tips that I can buy a new outfit too.

I head straight for the sequin dresses. Though I wear neutral clothing in my everyday life, I actually love to wear glittery bright clothes. I've had to hide so much of myself for most of my life, it's like I can breathe when I get to just be myself. I pull it out and it's freaking gorgeous.

Turning toward the counter, I ask the attendant. "Excuse me, can I get a dressing room?"

Giving me her best customer service smile, she replies. "Of course, follow me this way."

I hang up the dress on the hook and turn back toward her. "Thank you."

She starts to walk out of the stall then looks over her shoulder with a small smirk. "Let me know if you need anything else." Then she disappears behind the curtain, giving me my privacy.

As soon as my hands touch the fabric of the beautiful dress, the curtain opens. I pull the dress up to cover my body, "I'm still trying on this dress." I say quickly as I spin around to face them.

"Mia, what are you doing here?" I ask.

"What am I doing here? What are you doing here? You don't belong here, Ella."

"Mia, I'm not here to bother anyone. I just want to get a new dress."

Placing her hands on her hips, she asks, "What do you need a new dress for?"

"I'm going to the new club Midnight Blue with Suri."

She lets out a laugh that sounds more evil than jolly, "What do you think you'll be doing at the club? One look at you and your rags, everyone will know you aren't worth their time."

I clench my jaw trying to keep myself still. I don't want her to know that her words hurt. I take a few steps closer until we're only a few inches away. "You know, Mia, you don't have to be mean. We can be friends and I can help you with anything."

She flinches a tiny bit. I almost didn't catch it, but I know I'm getting to her in some way. I can't let her know that I found the ledger and pictures, but I do want her to know that I can help her if she wants it.

She steps into me then grabs my hair and uses it to pull me so close to her. "I don't know what you think you know but I won't ever need you or your help."

With those nasty words, she pushes me back away from her and walks out.

***

Later that night, I put on my new dress, which I did eventually try on and love, and I feel like a new woman. I put on the last touches of my makeup, I slip my shoes on and head out of the house toward the train station.

I get to the club right at nine just like I told Suri I would. I only have to wait a few minutes before she rolls up in a black car with her driver. When she pops out, I can't help but smile at her. She has her curly hair down, dressed in a modest black dress. "Suri, you look beautiful."

She doesn't say anything, but her cheeks redden. She is just the cutest little bookworm and has been by my side since we were young.

She wraps me in a tight hug. "Hey, stranger, it's been a long time since I've seen you,"

Letting out a sigh because I know she's right, I apologize. My whole life has been filled with work and what the step-witches want. "I know, I've been working a lot lately."

Suri claps her hands and with a grin she says, "Let's go let off some steam."

We walk into the club and our jaws drop. This place looks amazing. When I was here the other night, it was dark with a blue hue in every room making it hard to take in all of its features. Under the strobe lights and with the sound of the D.J., it just brings a different feel.

Both of us head straight to the bar to grab a drink before we let loose on the dance floor. We take a moment just to take in the atmosphere while we order drinks. It's crazy how different it feels to the masquerade party. Everyone here is dressed in their short, sparkly dresses. No gowns. No secrets. Just fun.

I take a sip of my drink. "Mmm...that's good," I tell Suri.

After a few sips, my body loosens up and I lean over to Suri practically yelling at her, "Want to dance?"

Suri nods at me, so I down my drink as we both place our glasses back on the bar and head straight for the middle of the dance floor. I just let my body take over at this point and refuse to think about anything else.

A man comes up behind Suri and they start dancing. I can tell that she's not one hundred percent comfortable, but she's smiling, and I know she needs this. I close my eyes to get lost in the music until I hear a growl in front of us.

What the fuck was that?

When I open my eyes, Brendan is standing in front of Suri talking to her. But behind them...

It's him.

My body starts to tremble being so close to him. The lust in his eyes as he looks at me pulls me in. Heat courses through me, my nipples harden, and my clit is throbbing. All I want to do is drown in him, but I can't seem to move. I just stand there dumbfounded. Not sure what to do next.

Thankfully, he recovers faster than me. Before I can even blink, he's standing in front of me. He grabs me behind my neck and pulls me to his lips. "Hello, baby girl. Daddy missed you."

Thirteen

Mikhail

Her body trembles as I speak directly into her ear. "Hello, baby girl. Daddy missed you."

My body heats with need as my cock starts to press against my zipper. I knew I missed her but I didn't realize how much. The absence has not cooled anything off between us, the chemistry is still there as much as it was the first night.

Moving her hair out of her face, I look into her deep blue eyes, and I can see that she feels this thing brewing between us. My mind drifts to the night we two had together. Shit, my cock is getting even harder. I need to get us out of here before I do something crazy.

Before Ella even can think about what is going to happen next, I wrap my arms around her shoulders and pull her into my body, making it easier to guide her through the maze of people on the dance floor and to the back of the club. Pausing at the bottom of the stairs of the VIP area, I beckon to Sergei that we are ready to leave. I don't even give her the option, she is leaving with me. He grabs another security guard and they both fall into sync with us. Making sure that we are protected, but more importantly, that she is protected..

Reaching the back exit, we pause for a beat in front of the large metal door. "How long until the car gets here?" I ask him.

"It should be pulling up now," Sergio answers.

My other security guy, who is standing on the other side of us, leans out of the door to check to see if the car has actually arrived. In my line of work, I can't be too careful. I don't need to be standing out in the open unnecessarily.

"The car is here, sir," he lets me know.

I release Ella's shoulders just long enough to rearrange her. Grabbing her wrist I pull her behind me as Sergei follows. I open the door for her and as soon as her butt hits the seat, I move in behind her.

I lean over Ella and grab the seatbelt making sure it's buckled. She just stares at me. I give her a wink. "Safety first."

She just shakes her head and smirks.

She's fucking adorable.

As all the doors to the car slam shut, Sergei confirms, "Your place?"

"Yes."

As we drive through the city, I look over at Ella. She's shivering. I place my hand on her arm as I ask, "Are you cold?"

She nods her head and whispers, "But also a little scared. I don't even know you."

I shrug off my coat and use it to drape across Ella like a blanket. "My name is Mikhail. You don't have to be scared of me. I would never hurt you."

Ella adjusts the coat but doesn't say anything. And even though I know the answer to my next question, I ask it anyways. "And what is your name, baby girl?"

She scoffs at me, like full on scoffs. "Don't pretend that you don't know my name. It's Ella."

I love her fire. But I see something else on her face, now that I'm looking closer. Her words sound strong but her body language says something completely different. She is plastered against the door, putting as much space between us as she can. I need her to know that she can trust me. I need to reassure her somehow so I place my hand on her thigh to help calm her.

"Everything is going to be okay, Ella," I say trying to reassure her but I don't want to push, so I don't say anything else.

But I continue to watch her and take in her reactions as we drive. Out of the corner of my eye, I can see her look down at my hand like she can't believe that I'm touching her.

If she only knew all the ways I want to touch her.

The SUV pulls up to my penthouse and I feel like a fucking kid at Christmas at the thought of Ella in my space.

Once we get the go ahead from Sergei that it's safe to exit, I pull Ella out of the car and walk straight to the secure elevator that goes to my penthouse.

Turning back toward Sergei, I say. "I don't want anyone to disturb me unless it's an emergency."

He nods, and I turn my attention back to the palm security reader. When the elevator doors open, I hurriedly enter with Ella by my side. "Only a select few have access to this elevator. You're safe here."

She doesn't respond to me, staying quiet the whole ride up to my penthouse. When the doors open, Ella gasps at the view, "This is beautiful."

"Not as beautiful as you."

Her pale skin blushes, and I wish I could see how far that blush goes. She continues to take in the room and I can't stop myself from trying to see the room through her eyes. The walls are bare with just a light gray paint on them, the furniture is modern and minimalist. The only piece in this room is an oversized black leather couch that sits right in front of a large T.V. I have no pictures, no knick knacks, nothing.

She turns to me with a question in her eyes. "Where are your memories?"

Pinching my brows, I ask her, "Memories?"

"You know, pictures and things that remind you of people and special times in your life?"

"I never had a reason to spend much time here, I spend most of it at the club. But now that I see you here, I think I was waiting for you."

I close the distance between us. When I'm close enough I reach out and lazily glide my hands down her arms until I'm holding her hands. "Why did you leave me that night?"

She sucks in a breath and looks down at the floor. She wasn't expecting me to ask her that, but she answers, "She would've punished me if she knew where I was. I wasn't supposed to be there."

What the actual fuck? Punish her?

Blood roars in my ears and I stop hearing what she said when she mentioned the word punishment. I try to keep my hands steady and my anger at bay. I don't need Ella thinking I'm mad at her. I mutter, "Who is she?"

"My step-mother. She doesn't like it when I disobey her," she replies with a glint in her eye and I take it she disobeys more than her step-mother knows.

"Tell me more," I demand.

"She married my dad after my mom died. She has two daughters and they were never kind to me but never out right mean… at least not in front of my dad. But when he got sick, the cruelty from her and my step-sisters increased. Now they treat me as if I'm their slave."

She lets out a breath. I can see the weight she's been carrying starts to lift. I stay quiet and let her work through her thoughts until she continues "I've been working hard to help save money so I can buy the house before my dad dies. The house was my mother's before she died."

As she speaks my anger increases and my whole body is shaking with it. How could anyone treat someone like that? My childhood might not have been the greatest but I never doubted that my dad cared for me on some level. My thoughts are reeling from all her revelations.

Suddenly, Ella reaches up and cups my face. "It's okay. I'm okay and I have a plan."

"You don't need a plan anymore. I'm here for you and I'll tear her and her daughters down to nothing," I curtly say.

She shakes her head. "You can't do that for me."

This fucking woman is crazy if she thinks I'm not going to do this for her. She seems to not understand that she's mine and has been since I saw her standing next to the bar that night.

"I will and no one will stop me." I lean down and crash my mouth to hers, showing her exactly how I feel.

Her phone vibrates in her purse. "Just ignore it," she says against my lips.

I keep kissing her, dipping my tongue into her sinful mouth. Her phone vibrates again, and she lets out a frustrated breath. "Just check it. I'll still be here when you're done."

Reluctantly letting me go, she walks over to the couch and picks up her purse to grab the phone. I use this moment to text Sergei.

> Me: Find everything you can on Ella's family, especially her step-mother.

> Sergei: On it.

Tucking my phone back into my pocket, I look over at the gorgeous woman who has restarted my frozen heart after all of these years.

Fourteen

Ella

Putting my phone back into my purse I turn around to find Mikhail leaning against the doorway to the kitchen staring at me.

"Everything okay?"

"Yeah it was just my friend making sure I'm okay."

Reaching for me he pulls me into his chest, giving me a chaste kiss on the lips. "And are you okay?"

With a soft smile, I drape my arms around his neck. I lean up on my tippy toes and give him my own kiss on his beautiful pouty lips, whispering, "I'm perfect."

Tightening his arms against me, he uses his tongue to coax my mouth open. I need to feel him. I need to feel his skin against mine. I move my hands down to his shirt and rub them against his hard chest before I start unbuttoning his shirt. When I finally get them undone, I caress my hands over his shoulders, pushing his shirt to the ground. He's just as exquisite as I remember.

I kiss my way down his chest but before I can get too low, Mikhail grips my hair pulling my head back to look into my eyes. He drags his rough finger down over my dress until he gets to the hem of my dress. Pulling up my dress, he pushes my thong to the side and he slowly starts to tease my clit. But I need more, I need him.

As he rubs his fingers through my folds, I groan. "More."

Mikhail kisses my neck and says, "Don't worry, Daddy has you."

He lifts me up into his arms and my legs instantly wrap around his waist. We continue to kiss as he carries us down a hallway into the bedroom. He tosses me on the huge, soft bed, and I land on my back spread out just for him.

He crawls up my body between my spread thighs and hovers over me, asking, "Are you ready for me, baby girl?"

"Yes," I answer enthusiastically as my legs open wider to give him more access. It feels so right deep in my bones. I have never been so ready for anything in my life.

Smacking my inner thigh, I yelp with the sensation, but I can feel my pussy getting wetter, especially when he demands. "Yes, what?"

I know what he wants and I don't want to make him wait. "Yes, Daddy," I purr.

He rubs my inner thighs where he smacked me, followed by kisses, whispering, "That's my good girl."

I'm ruined. No one will ever be able to compare to him. Mikhail pulls my dress up over my head, throwing it to the ground. His hands slide down the front of my body and he pulls my underwear until there is a ripping sound. *Did he just rip my panites?* He grabs my thighs and stares. "What a beautiful pink pussy. From now on, it belongs to me, Ella."

I nod my head in agreement because I can't seem to find my words. I've never felt like this before, like I'm beautiful. He pulls me down the bed and closer to him, "Words, baby."

"Yes. I belong to you, Daddy."

"That's right. No one will ever touch this pussy or any part of you again. Do you understand?"

A ball of emotion forms in my throat. I don't say anything because if I tried to speak right now, I would start to cry. And I don't want to cry right now. I push back my tears and relax into him.
And I let myself just feel.

Mikhail must see the emotion on my face no matter how hard I've tried pushing it back. He leans down softly kissing my clit. "You are so beautiful, Ella, and I will spend the rest of my days worshiping you."

Before I can respond, he spears his tongue inside of me then fucks my pussy with his mouth. "Fuck...that feels so good."

Clutching the sheets as hard as possible, I try to thrust up into him, but he pushes my hips down making me feel all of it. Then he sucks my clit, and I come so hard I swear I see stars.

"Baby girl, open your eyes," he whispers. I open them and he's right there. Looking at me. Seeing all of me. Then he kisses me, and I can taste myself on him. It feels so dirty but so good.

"That was one. Are you ready for more, baby girl?"

Nodding enthusiastically, I reach to grab his pants when he takes my hand. "This is about you."

"I want to taste you. You wouldn't deny me?"

He grins at me. "I would never deny you anything."

Getting up on his knees he drops his pants and boxers releasing his huge cock. I can see the precum dripping from the tip. I lick my lips and he growls.

He. Growls.

Crawling up my body, he traps me underneath him straddling my shoulders where I can only rise up a small bit.

"Do you want to taste my cock?"

"Yes, Daddy. Give it to me."

I gag instantly when he thrusts his cock into my mouth. It takes me a minute to adjust to his large cock at this angle but I've never been more excited. I can feel my juices drip down my thighs and more with every thrust.

I hum around his cock and make sure I rub against the vein that runs down his cock before swirling my tongue around the tip. His thrusts become more erratic like he's about to come but he suddenly pulls out. I give him a pout before I can stop myself.

He moves down until we're face to face. His chest heaving and he gives me a pointed look, towering over me. "When I come, it will be in your pussy."

"Then put your cock in my pussy."

And where the fuck did that come from?

I don't usually talk like that, but this man brings out a whole new side of me. He seems to give me more confidence. Makes me feel safe and desirable.

"That's exactly what I'm going to do," he says while he grabs my hips so hard, I bet I'll have fingerprint bruises on them. Lining up his cock with my pussy, he slams into me.

"Shit, Ella, you're so fucking tight. Your pussy is already strangling my cock."

I've never been able to orgasm with just penetration, but I'm so close. "I'm c...close." I groan.

"Get there, Ella. Give it to me, baby."

He lifts himself up on his knees a little bit more, changing the angle slightly, and holy fuck. Only a couple thrusts later, I tighten around him, and I'm coming bringing him along with me. This time, I'm pretty sure I black out from the intensity.

When I open my eyes, Mikhail has a warm wet rag between my legs. "As much as I want to see my cum running down your leg, I thought you might feel more comfortable if I clean you up."

I just hum in contentment, I feel so tired, happy. I could sleep forever after that. He snuggles in behind me, both of us still naked and pulls me tight into him covering us with blankets. Kissing my temple, he whispers, "Go to sleep, baby girl."

And I do knowing I want to stay in this dream forever. I don't want to leave and go back to reality.

Fifteen

Mikhail

The sun shines through the window illuminating the whole room. I roll away from the light and groan. I'm not ready to get up yet. My eyes snag on the spot next to me and I can't help but stare at the stunning woman lying there. She's on her stomach giving me the perfect view of her back and the side of her breast that is peeking out from underneath her. The sheet is draped down around her waist covering up her beautiful ass and one of her long lean legs while the other is sticking out.

I gently rub my fingertips down her spine. She moans and rolls over to face me. Slowly, she opens her eyes as her pink lips slide into a smile…mmm… "Good morning, Mikhail."

My chest tightens with the way my name rolls off her lips. Could this be what it's really like for the rest of our lives? Waking up next to a gorgeous woman, hearing her shout my name at the top of her lungs every morning. *This is what I want.*

"Good morning, baby."

"Why are you already up? I thought old men needed their sleep," she says with a wink.

I chuckle and shit, I don't even remember the last time I laughed. "Oh I'll show you what older men need." Gripping her thigh, I lean down to her lips. "You're gonna pay for that."

Then I go in for a kiss but pull back at the last minute with a grin.

"Hey," she whines.

Pulling away from her I bounce off the bed. "Get up," I tell her while I grab a pair of boxers and joggers from the dresser, putting them on.

She pulls the sheet up over her head groaning while she turns over, exposing more of her peachy ass.

"Nope. I want to sleep in."

"Well, you can when you get old," I say, smacking her ass. "Get up and I'll make you breakfast."

With that last request, I head out the bedroom door toward the kitchen. I want to take care of her, feed her, buy her whatever she needs. It's obvious that Ella takes care of everyone but herself, and that stops now. This woman has the weight of the world on her shoulders. It's plain as day to see. I want her to let me help. I want her to know she's not alone anymore.

I don't cook much but one thing my mom made sure I knew how to make was pancakes and bacon. Let's hope she likes pancakes.

Grabbing out a pan from the cabinet, I place it on the stove and move to the pantry. I grab all the ingredients and measure it out into the mixing bowl.

I preheat the oven and put the bacon on the baking sheet, then place them in the oven. That's when I hear Ella's sexy, sleepy, morning voice.

"Bacon...in the oven?"

I look over my shoulder and my heart starts to pound. She is standing at the entry of my kitchen in one of my old shirts and a pair of my boxers. Her face is clear of makeup and I can see the freckles that dust her nose. Her chestnut brown hair is thrown haphazardly into a messy bun on top of her head and I don't think I have ever seen a more gorgeous woman.

The caveman inside of me wants to just throw her over my shoulder and chain her to my bed, but I turn back to the oven, needing to remember what she really needs and what I really want to give her. Not just sex...everything.

"Yep. My mom taught me this when I was a kid. If you bake the bacon, it helps keep the mess to a minimum."

She moves to the bar as I start to cook the pancakes. "Are you close with your mom?"

"My mom died when I was in high school," I reply.

Her voice softens, "I'm sorry, Mikhail. I know what it's like to lose a parent. What about your dad? Are you close with him?"

My face softens with her words remembering what she told me last night about her mom and dad. I think hard about her question. I'm not not close with my dad. We meet up every week to discuss work, but we don't really dive into anything too deep.

"Growing up my dad was strict. He's a second generation Russian immigrant who works hard. We are not as close as we could be, but we're there for each other."

Not wanting to get more into my family dynamics, because I'm not sure how she will take everything, I make her a plate of pancakes then place it in front of her.

Lifting her plate up to her nose, she says, "Mmm...this smells good."

Then the timer on the oven goes off. "Just in time." I say with a wink.

I grab the bacon out of the oven and serve her two pieces. "Eat," I tell her.

As Ella eats, I make my plate and join her. We eat in a comfortable silence and it feels like this was always meant to be. When I hear the clanging of her silverware, I look up and Ella is getting up to leave. I grab her arm and pull her onto my lap. "Where are you going?"

She licks her lips and my eyes follow the movement. And I can't help it. I lean forward and lick her lips too. She tastes like maple syrup and bacon and Ella and I want more of that right now.

Moving all the plates to the side, I press Ella against the edge of the counter. "You know, baby girl, I never gave you a proper punishment."

She turns to look at me with those doe-like eyes, pulling her bottom lip in between her teeth, worrying. I grip her thighs with my hands leaning in. "Don't worry, you'll like this punishment."

She just stares at me.

"Yes or no, baby girl?"

"Yes," she whispers.

"That's my good girl."

I push her until the front of her is flush with the counter top, then I pull down the boxers, exposing her ass to me. I smack it once, reveling in the pink that it brings to her skin. "Mmm...dessert for breakfast."

Before she can even respond to my retort, I drop to my knees and spread her wide. I lick her from clit to hole. Her legs muscles stiffen. "Mikhail, what are you doing?"

"Relax. Daddy has you," I answer as I rub the globes of her ass.

Her legs start to loosen a little bit, and I lick her pussy until my face drips with her. I collect her juices with my index finger and swirl it around her back hole, then I slowly dip my finger into it, while my tongue massages her clit. "Ahh...Daddy."

As she climbs higher and higher her tight hole sucks in my finger. I add another one, to help stretch her out. She's done it before and she's going to take my fat cock in her tight ass.

When she explodes all over my face, I take my fingers out of her ass, and quickly stand up and pull my cock out of my boxers. I push into her tight hole willing myself to go slow so I don't hurt her too much. When I hit the ring of resistance, I continue pushing forward slowly, when Ella snaps at me, "Faster, Mikahil. Harder."

Thank Christ

With one hard thrust, I'm fully seated. I kiss her lower back. "You're doing so good, baby girl, taking Daddy's cock in your tight ass."

Gritting her teeth, she softens a bit, "Daddy, it feels good. But I need you to move."

I start rocking in and out of her while she rubs her clit. *Mine.* Her body molds to mine and she takes me with such ease. *Mine.* I don't give a fuck about anyone else. Ella. Will. Be. Mine. She will have my children and I will remove anyone who stands in our way.

"Fuck, Ella, I'm so close. Make sure you keep rubbing that sweet spot for me."

"Mikhail," She moans something else that's incoherent. I love that she's so caught up in the moment. Her body starts to tighten and my balls pull up. Grunting, I let go and spill my cum into her sweet ass. Panting and trying to catch my breath, I lean over her, resting my head on her shoulder. Giving her small kisses. "Ella, that was so incredible."

"Yes, it was. And as much as I would love to sit here with you, I really need to clean up," she says as she tries to push me off a little. I don't really move but I get the hint. I straighten back up and I pull out of her. My cum starts to leak out of her ass and down her leg. "Shit, I like seeing me run down your leg. Are you sure you need to clean up?"

Ella looks over her shoulder giving me a grin. "Yes, Mikhail. I can't walk around with cum running down my leg."

She walks past me and heads toward the bathroom. When she's done, she grabs her phone. Looking at a message, her face pales.

"Are you okay?" I ask as I come up on her.

"Umm...I got a message from my step-mother and she needs me at home."

"No, you can't go. It's not safe."

"Mikhail, I have to go home. I can't lose everything I've been working for. I have a plan. Besides, I can handle whatever she throws at me."

"If you insist, then I will take you."

"No. I don't need you to come with me."

"It's non-negotiable. I'll take you home. And I'm going to have eyes on the house at all times."

She stares deep in my face for a long time. At some point she must realize that I'm serious because her shoulders sag a bit when she whispers, "Okay."

She collects her stuff and we head down to the parking lot and get in my car. We stay silent the whole time we drive. When we pull up, I order, "Stay here." I get out and run over to her side so I can open the door for her.

When she gets out, I give her a kiss on her cheek. "I'll come get you tomorrow night to take you to dinner."

"Mikhail, I come with a lot of baggage."

"I don't give a fuck if you come with a whole luggage store, you are mine. I will come by tomorrow night and we will go to dinner. Do you hear me, Ella?"

"Yes."

"I will text you later, but if anything happens, text me."

"But you don't have my number and I don't have yours."

"Are you sure about that? Check your phone, baby girl." I tell her with a wink.

Ella pulls out her phone and giggles. Patting my chest she says, "You are something else, Mikhail."

"You have no idea."

Her eyes are drawn to a window in the front of the house when she says with a hint of fear in her voice, "I better go."

She leaves me standing there as she disappears into the house, I just stay there... staring. Worrying. Even with all my self assurance, power, and connections, I have a bad feeling about letting her enter that house.

Sixteen

Ella

I walk into the house with a sense of dread sitting in my stomach. I close the front door as quietly as possible, so I have a moment to get my bearings before I see any of them. I didn't tell Mikhail but the text I got from my step-mother was not warm and fuzzy. In fact, it scared me a bit. I can still see it in my head as plain as day,

> Step-Mother: Ella get your ass home. If you aren't here in one hour you will never see your father again.

Making my way up the stairs to my room, I can hear my heartbeat in my ears. I've never stayed out like this before. I push the boundaries but not like this. Something about Mikhail made me bold. Made me forget that my life is a wreck, and that I don't even have ownership over it.

When I make it up to my room, I finally let out a breath. At least in this room I have some type of safety, surrounded by the things that help me feel grounded. Things that bring me happy memories of a family that loved each other.

Until I see my step-mother sitting on my bed. She has a stern look on her face. Staring at me, looking deep down in my soul. I've always hated that about her, it's like she can see your weakness right away and use it against you.

I don't even attempt to move.

Looking me up and down with disgust, she sneers at me, "Are you a whore now, Ella? Were you out all night spreading your legs?"

I bristle but I don't bother addressing it. I can't take her bait. If I do, my plan will go up in flames, so I calmly answer her. "I'm sorry that I was out all night without letting you know step-mother. I was with Suri."

She stands up from my bed looking at me. "I thought you were smarter than lying to me Ella. I know you weren't with Suri. I saw who dropped you off. Do you even know who he is?"

I just keep staring at her, staying silent and keeping my mask in place. I can't let her know that she is getting to me. She lets out a humorless laugh, "Of course you don't know who that is? You naive girl.

That's Mikhail Sokolov, the heir to the Bratva. A notorious playboy. He's ten years older than you and will use you up and spit you out."

By the time, she finishes her chest is heaving, and she just stares at me, but I know that she's not done. Marching toward me she grabs my arms and starts shaking me. "I won't have you whore yourself out to him. You will not ruin this family because of this. I have a good thing going."

"I'm not his whore, we belong together," comes out of my mouth before I can stop it. Shit, why did I say that? Now she knows I have feelings for him. This is not good.

An evil look comes over her face and the worry I was feeling before deepens. Now I'm completely frightened. "You are fucking stupid, Ella. You will not see him again," she says as she tightens her fingers on my arms, hard enough that I will have bruises.

"You won't be able to keep us apart. He won't let you," I scream.

"Watch me," she violently says as she pushes me back. The force from the push causes me to crash into the nightstand sitting behind me.

Damn it. That fucking hurt. My back is burning where I landed. I keep my head down taking in deep breaths, trying to stifle the pain that I'm feeling at the possibility of not seeing Mikhail and the physical pain that I feel in my back. But I refuse to cry or show any more emotion than I already have.

I hear her footsteps move away from me and I look up to brace myself. She looks back at me while bending down and grabbing my purse. "No. You can't take my purse. I need my stuff to work tonight," I say as I try to get up from the floor, stumbling with pain.

"You won't be going to work tonight. Actually, you won't be going anywhere. You will stay up here in your room until the next auction."

I'm fucking dumbfounded. She thinks that she will put me in the auction. No fuck that. I won't be like my step-sisters. Moving as fast as I can to the door, I lunge to grab her but don't make it in time. She closes the door in my face. Grabbing the knob, I try to pull it open, but before I can, I hear the deafening click of the lock.

Banging on the door, I yell, "Let me out. You won't get away with this."

Tears start to stream down my face, but I continue to yell and scream hoping someone will let me out until my throat is raw. The fight leaves me. Crawling over to my bed, I climb in, look up at the ceiling, and cry.

How the hell did my life become like this? My thoughts drift to Mikhail, and my heart hurts so much with the idea of never seeing him again. She said he was the heir to the Bratva, and even though he didn't say anything to me about it, I can feel in my bones that she isn't lying.

Mikhail has a layer of danger underneath his charming smile. I saw it the first time I laid eyes on him, but I've had danger lurking in the background my whole life. His danger doesn't scare me. If anyone should be worried, it should be my step-mother.

Mikhail told me that I belong to him and I'm going to trust in him. He will find me, help me get out of here, and then we will destroy my step-mother together.

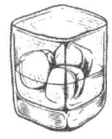

Seventeen

Mikhail

It's been twenty four hours since I've seen or heard from Ella, and I feel sick to my stomach. I check my messages for the hundredth time, still no response.

I sent a text to Ella almost immediately after I left her last night. I re-read the text again just to make sure that I haven't missed anything.

> Me: Hey, baby girl, how are you?

> Me: How was work?

> Me: Ella why haven't you responded, you should be off work by now.

> Me: I'm worried, please answer me.

> Me: Ella, you better answer me.

The last one I sent was about an hour ago... and nothing.

Me: I will be at your house at seven you better be ready.

I've never felt like this. I can feel it deep in my gut; something is wrong. Even though I haven't known her for long, this feels out of character. I've been arguing with myself all day, going back and forth if I should go over there and confront her.

"Fuck it. I'm going over there," I mutter under my breath.

When I pull up in front of her house, all the bad feelings I had earlier grow. I sit in my car for a few minutes, analyzing everything. It looks the same as it did yesterday. From the outside it's cute and homey, a normal looking house in a normal looking neighborhood. But right now, it feels a little bit more sinister, feeding that feeling that something is wrong.

The house is silent, no movement, no lights, nothing. Taking a deep breath, I walk up to the front door and knock, expecting Ella to answer. I'm surprised when a dark-haired woman who looks to be about the same age answers and damn, she looks slightly familiar. Where have I seen her before? "Hello, can I help you?" she asks, looking somewhat confused.

Clearing my throat, I make sure to keep my body relaxed. "Yes, I'm here for Ella."

Her brows draw in, causing her lips to go into a straight line. "She's not here right now."

I push my way more into the entryway, causing her to lose her grip with the front door. "I'll wait."

"Okay," she says in a meek quiet voice. Then turns to lead me into a living room. Pointing to the couch, she says, "You can sit there. Can I get you a drink?"

I make myself comfortable. "No, thank you." She goes to leave but I blurt out, "What is your name?"

She keeps her gaze down and doesn't look at me but answers, "Leah." Then the young woman leaves without another word. As I sit there in silence, I take in the room. The walls look to have some character, but the furniture doesn't seem to fit. It seems gaudy and showy.

A few minutes later another woman who looks similar to the one who answered the door, but this one seems to have a darker quality about her. She doesn't speak at first but moves over to me, swinging her hips back and forth as she does, never breaking eye contact. "Hello, Mikhail," she purrs at me.

This time I'm the confused one, I don't think I've ever met this woman before. "I'm sorry, but do I know you?"

She leans over to make sure I get a full view down her shirt and drags her nail across the stubble on my jawline. My jaw tightens with the touch. "Everyone knows the great Mikhail Sokolov."

Trying not to recoil, I narrow my eyes at this woman. I grit my teeth and snap at her, "Don't touch me."

She flinches a tiny bit but goes to touch me again. I quickly grab her wrist. Gritting my teeth, I release her. As she stumbles back, I say. "I won't ask you again. Now, tell me where Ella is?"

Waving her arms in a dismissive manner she goes to sit on the couch across from me. "Who knows where Ella is? She's always making her way around the city, spreading her legs wherever she goes."

My hands clench on my lap trying not to snap this woman's neck for talking about Ella like that. I take a slow breath, making sure I'm relaxed before I speak next. The woman seems to take it as permission to keep speaking. "Ella has always been the flake of the family. Getting in trouble, sleeping around with all the wrong men. You know she didn't really have a mother to teach her better."

A stern voice interrupts us, "Mia, that is enough. Our guest doesn't care about the nighttime activities of your step-sister."

We both turn our heads to see an older woman that resembles the one sitting in front of me standing at the entryway of the living room.

The older woman continues, "Now, Mia, why don't you go check on everything upstairs?"

With orders from the older woman, the younger one gets up leaving the room. Ella's step-mother taps her fingers on the chair silently studying me. I'm not sure what she thinks she'll find, but I've been trained since a young age to not give anything away. This woman is trying to keep my baby girl from me, and I will not allow that to happen. I will kill her before I allow anything to happen to Ella.

Eighteen

Mikhail

We sit in the living room staring at each other, but I don't say anything. My father always said that if you sit in silence long enough, many people will reveal their secrets to you. If they don't...watch your back.

I use this time to examine the woman in front of me, the one who has tormented Ella since she was a little girl. She looks even more familiar than the younger woman. Have I encountered her before in a business deal? Racking my brain, I try to remember where I could've seen her.

She is the first to break the silence between us, and I smirk a little feeling like I won. But then she says something that surprises me, but I don't let it show. "I've met your father. He's a very powerful man."

Nodding my head, I wonder where she's going with this. Is she connected to my father somehow? Maybe she works for him? I don't take her bait but don't totally redirect the conversation, I just simply state the obvious. "There are lots of powerful men in this city."

"Yes, there is, but your father is the most powerful. And what would he say if all his secrets are released to the public, just because you couldn't leave some girl alone."

The underlying threat hangs between us. Shit, this woman has balls. Of course I don't give a fuck about what she thinks she knows, because I can guarantee that she doesn't know anything. My father holds all of his cards close to his chest and doesn't believe in showing them until necessary.

I casually throw my arm across the back of the couch. Time to fuck with this bitch. "Is that so? Do you think that would be the smart move on your part? As you say, my father is the most powerful man in the city...I wonder what he would do if he found the person who released information about him," I say as I whistle.

Her face pales at my words and now I know she didn't think this through. But then she seems to gain some courage because she whispers, "You know I told her."

"Told her what?"

"I told her that you're the heir of the Bratva and that you would use and discard her."

My jaw ticks as anger starts to envelop me.

"She didn't take it very well. It was obvious you didn't tell her. Do you think she'll forgive you for lying to her?"

"What happens between me and her is none of your concern."

I'm done with this woman, and I start to think of all the ways I could get rid of her, when my phone buzzes in my pocket.

Sergei's name flashes on my screen. I look up at the older woman, excusing myself. "I have to take this. Don't move."

"Of course." I can tell my command pisses her off but she's smart enough to know not to say anything else.

I turn and walk into the hallway by the front door answering the phone. "Sergei."

"Are you with Ella?" He sounds a bit distressed which has the hairs on the back of my neck standing up. Surprised by his question, I draw my eyebrows together as I answer him. "I'm at her house. According to her family she isn't here, but something doesn't feel right."

I don't expand any further knowing Sergei will read between the lines and give me what I need. He doesn't say anything for so long that I check to make sure my phone is connected. He knows something and is trying to figure out how to tell me. I can feel it.

"Sergei, what do you know?" I demand.

"I just sent a few pictures to your phone. After doing more investigating on Ella, I found this woman who connected to her."

Looking down at my phone, I check the text he sent me. I knew she looked familiar. I'm staring back at the pictures of the older woman who was just sitting in front of me, talking, kissing and fucking some of the most powerful men that attend my masquerade ball. The same men who came to me a few days after the auction, claiming that I was taking advantage of them. Luring them in and using women to blackmail them for money. They were angry and rightfully so.

"She must be the one who has been fleecing the guests from the auctions. The woman could become desperate if she thinks you're on to her."

"She doesn't yet. But I'll take care of it. Send me a few men. Tell them to sit out front until they see my signal."

"Got it, boss. And Mikhail… be careful."

"Always." I hang up and stare at my phone trying to come up with a plan. The most important thing is finding Ella, and then I'll turn this woman over to my father.

It's one thing to come after me, but to come after my woman, my Bratva, and my business. That is unforgivable. I return back to the living room ready to make this woman pay.

I sit back down on the couch, back straight, leg spread making myself seem larger. I assess the woman in front of me. She could be attractive if she wasn't a manipulating bitch. Leaning forward, I ask, "Did you think you would get away with it?"

Her lips thin with my question, I can tell that she's irritated by my question. "I'm not sure I know what you mean."

"Are you sure that's the answer you want to give me?"

She stays still, not giving me anything away. Not answering. "Okay, let's play it your way then."

Grabbing my phone, I pull up the pictures that Sergei sent me of her and place them on the table in front of her. "Would you like to explain?"

I continue as I swipe back and forth through them, giving her a clear view of the proof that I'm showing her. She keeps her eyes on the photos and I can see the wheels turning as she tries to figure out her next move. When her eyes meet mine, I can tell she's made a choice of how she is going to handle it, and then seals it with her words.

"What am I looking at? I'm not doing anything different than any other guests at the masquerade ball," she asks with a shrug, trying to be nonchalant.

Pointing down at the pictures, I respond. "The difference being that these men have come to me accusing me of taking advantage of them while they are in my club under my protection."

Leaning in a little closer to her, I whisper, "And you and I both know that I didn't take advantage of them."

Relaxing back on the couch, I let the information I give her settle in the air. She opens her mouth but before she can spew any type of lies, I hold my hand up stopping her.

"I will give you this, you were careful. We've been investigating for a couple of years now, but your time has come to an end."

"You're mistaken. This is not proof. This is just proof that I've had sex with them. I never took advantage of anyone."

I grab my knife from the inside pocket of my suit jacket. To the world I'm a charming man that knows exactly how to talk to people and in life that has served well. But when someone crosses me, I show them who I really am, a man who will do anything for what he wants.

And right now what I want is Ella.

Rubbing my knife across the back of my hand, I harden my voice. "Listen. I know you did it and that's the only proof that matters. Since you took advantage of guests at a Bratva establishment, we consider it a betrayal. Now, you're going to tell me where Ella is. If you don't, I will kill you and your daughters for everything."

Her body goes still, and the color from her face drains completely. "She's upstairs. In her room."

Shooting to my feet, I push everything out of my way and run up the stairs. The need to get to her is overwhelming. Loud voices fill the hallway and I follow them. When I reach Ella's room, I quietly enter the room. Taking in the scene that is before me, my blood turns to ice.

No, this can't be happening.

My heart pounds in my chest.

Ella is sitting up on the edge of the bed looking as if she might stand up, but Leah quickly moves in front of Ella. Holding her shoulder down with her hand, keeping her in place. Without any warning, Leah smacks Ella in the face.

I start to take a step, but Leah is screaming at Ella before I can move. "Do you know what you did?"

Ella is shaking her head and I barely hear her whisper. "I don't know what you are talking about Leah."

Suddenly, Ella's head whips around and she screams in pain. My hands instantly clench. I don't move this time though because Leah starts to confess her sins, "You had to go and spread your legs for him. You ruined everything and now you're going to pay."

Leah starts to wave a gun then settles it on Ella's head. Oh fuck no. This is not happening, I tip toe into the room keeping to the shadows by the door.

I hear a gun cocking and then Ella starts to plead for her life, "Leah, you don't want to do that?"

But Leah doesn't answer.

"Leah, you don't want to kill me. This isn't you."

She tsks. "Oh step-sister, you don't know me. In fact I'm not sure anyone has ever known me. Everyone always thinks Mia or Mother is in charge when in fact it's always been me."

Leah gives a little cackle, with no humor, and it's pure evil.

"What did you think would happen? Everything was going as planned and then you had to ruin it all. Mother and I were going to be rich, and we were going to leave you and Mia to deal with the fallout. Everyone would have believed it too. Mia has always been an entitled little bitch, leaving no doubt that she would do anything to get ahead. But no, you had to get involved. I know you found the ledger, and you know that we've been taking money from the guests at Midnight Blue. Now you will pay. I'm going to kill you and convince him that Mia did it. And that Mia is the one who had the idea to take money from the men at the auction."

She starts to pace back and forth in the room, muttering out loud, "If I don't kill you and convince Mikhail that it was you and Mia, then he will kill all of us. Yes, that's what I will do. I've kept my secret this long, no one will suspect me."

Ella looks up at her step-sister with tears running down her face. The closer I get to them, I see the bruise starting to form on her cheek. The hatred that I feel right now is beyond anything I have ever felt before. It's time to end this. I've heard enough. Moving from the shadows, I pull my gun from my waistband and I don't waste any time. I shoot the woman who dared to threaten what belongs to me in the back of her head.

Nineteen

Ella

Leah's eyes swing to me with an intense look of hatred. Tears are running down my face.

Closing my eyes, I ready myself to face the music. Images of my mother, father and Mikhail cross my lids. I see my mother and I baking in the kitchen. Dad and I playing in the backyard. The future I could've had with Mikhail. I imagine what my wedding to him would've been like. What our children would've looked like.

I take a deep breath knowing that I'm about to see my mother again. A loud gunshot goes off. I expect to feel the bite of the bullet, but it never comes. When I open my eyes, that's when I see Leah laying down on the ground with blood surrounding her. What the hell happened?

One minute she was about to kill me and now she is dead.

Someone grabs my cheek, turning me away from Leah's body. And I'm staring into deep brown eyes that I thought I would never see again. Mikhail. My heart skips a beat. He's here. He came for me. "You saved me. You k-killed her."

His face softens a bit as he leans his head onto my forehead, "There is nothing I wouldn't do to keep you safe, baby girl."

We both just stare at each other as the room falls away. He leans forward cradling my head to give me a chaste kiss. When he pulls back, there is blood on his hand.

"Mikhail, I don't feel very good."

"Don't move. Let me call a doctor. You got hit pretty hard." Then he glances over his shoulder "And someone to clean this up."

Pulling out his phone, he makes a few texts. "Let's get you out of here. The doctor will meet us at the penthouse."

A loud noise from downstairs makes my body stiffen. "Don't worry, it's just my men," he whispers.

"You've got men who deal with this stuff?" I ask.

"We'll talk about that later when you're feeling better."

"But..."

I don't have time to ask him anything because Mikhail lifts me, cradling me to his chest as we make our way downstairs.

I don't see much except the furniture thrown haphazardly around the room. Mia and my step-mother cower in the corner as Mikhail's men surround them.

Mikhail moves quickly out the door and into a waiting car. My eyes start to feel heavy. Laying my head against his chest, I can hear and feel his heartbeat. He's here. He came for me. I'm so tired.

I feel a kiss against my temple as my eyes start to close. "It's okay, baby girl, get some rest. We'll be home soon."

My body drifts off to sleep, dreaming about a life and future that I never thought I could have before.

Twenty

Ella

My eyes flutter open and I look around. I recognize that I'm in Mikhail's room. How did I get to his penthouse? The memories of the last twenty-four hours play in my mind. My step-mother accusing me of being a whore, locking me in my room. Telling me that she was going to put me in an auction. Leah trying to kill me, and then Mikhail. Mikhail coming to save me.

Then I remember the ledger I had found in Mia's room. I need to tell Mikhail. I go to get up but my head starts to pound. A deep voice next to me says, "Whoa, be careful, Ella. You need to rest."

"No, I need to tell you something but my head hurts," I say, grabbing his wrist.

"It's okay, Ella. We can talk about it later. The doctor said you need as much rest as possible."

"Please, Mikhail."

"Baby girl, why don't you rest a little bit more, then you can tell me. How about that?" he asks as he pulls me into his chest. The warmth of his body envelops me, and my body gets heavy.

"Okay, maybe just for a little bit longer."

A deep chuckle comes from behind me as sleep takes me under.

The next time I wake, sunlight pours in through the window. I roll over to look for Mikhail but he's gone. I feel around in his space, but it's cold. I instantly panic. Did he leave? Is something wrong?

I rush out of the room and relief hits me when I see him sitting on the couch in the living room. I lick my lips as I take in the scene. Casually sitting there, looking at his phone, dressed in black joggers, and a tight white T-shirt that clings to every muscle on his body.

My nipples pebble and my clit starts to throb at just the sight of this man. This man who would do anything for me. Fuck, I want to ride him into the sunset. As if he could read my dirty thoughts he looks up and gives me a grin. "Good morning, baby girl. You look like you're feeling a little better."

He puts his phone down on the coffee table then pats his lap. "Come sit on Daddy's lap."

I don't delay. I obey walking toward him, falling down on his lap. I giggle as I catch myself with my arms wrapped around his neck. I give him a kiss, deepening it, trying to show him what I'm feeling. I don't know how he did it but he stole my heart and I don't want it back. Without skipping a beat, he continues to kiss me as he pulls my shirt up over my head.

When he pulls back, he leans his forehead against mine as he draws his finger across my collar bone and down to my breasts. "You know you scared me yesterday, Ella. And I don't like being scared."

My cheeks burn from his touch on my body as he continues his exploration. Circling his fingers around my nipples, I arch into him and moan. "Hmm...I need you."

"You need me?"

"Yes."

"I don't know. You took a pretty good hit to your head. I want to make sure you're okay."

"Mikhail, I'm fine." I snap at him. "I need you more. I thought I would never see you again. Please give me what I need."

My words must spur him into action because he pulls his cock out of his joggers and lines it up with my core. With one thrust he's inside my pussy, stretching me deliciously, and I love it.

"That feels so good, Mikhail."

"I know, baby. Take my cock, ride me," he demands as he smacks my ass.

I start bouncing up and down on him as he grabs my hips. He stops me then pulls me forward so my clit rubs against his pubic bone as he starts to thrust hard up into me.

"Shit. Fuck me harder."

Mikhail doesn't miss a step. He picks up his game and pounds into me from underneath and my pussy flutters as I climb toward my orgasm. He dips his head down capturing my nipples in his mouth tugging with his teeth, and that does it for me. I clench down on him and explode taking him with me.

Once we have calmed down, Mikhail smacks my ass again commanding, "Don't ever scare me again like that, Ella."

"Of course, Daddy."

I look up at Mikhail, "I need to talk to you."

"Okay, tell me."

"After we slept together at the club, I found a ledger along with photos in Mia's bedroom."

He nods as he listens to my words, then he surprises me with his next words. "Were these photos of them with men?"

"Yes. How did you know?" I ask, confused.

"We've been aware of someone stealing money from our guests at the club but wasn't sure who it was until yesterday. Your step-mother and step-sister would participate in the auction, then get these men in compromising positions, taking pictures of them, ignoring the rules and blackmailing the men into giving them money or they would release the photos."

"But how?"

"Do you know who my father is?" he asks.

"I recall my step-mother saying something about the Bratva."

"Yes, my father is the Pakhan which means he's in charge and is very dangerous. He has unlimited means to find out information and I was using his connections to look into it. What she was doing was bad for business and needed to be dealt with."

I take in his words. Fuck, what was my step-mother thinking stealing from the Bratva. Did she know? "What will happen to my step-mother and step-sisters?"

Mikhail doesn't back away from my question, he answers it with complete honesty. "Well, Leah is dead. Your step-mother will have to pay for her betrayal against the Bratva with her life. But Mia seems to not be aware of the real plan that they had, she was just jealous and doing her mother's bidding. I ordered her to leave the city and never return. It's over, Ella."

I collapse in his arms sobbing. Is it really over? Rubbing my back, he comforts me, "You don't have to worry anymore, Ella. I will keep you safe."

And I know he is right. He will do everything in his power to keep me safe. I pull back looking at him and whisper, "I love you."

His eyes twinkle with his reply, "I love you, too."

Twenty-One

Mikhail

A few days after everything went down with Ella and her family, things between us settled back into whatever can be considered normal. The only thing I don't like is that I'm living here at my penthouse and she's living at her house. She should be with me, but she's been refusing to move in. Well, I have news for her, we will be living together...soon. I grin while I grab my keys.

Pulling up in front of her house, it's encapsulated in darkness. Grabbing my bag from the back of the car, I use my key to go inside. No one is home, which is exactly what I need.

Ella is still working at The Tower despite my protests. I've told her over and over again that she doesn't need to work, but she argues with me. Always claiming something about wanting to be independent.

I've made sure we don't have anymore threats lurking over us. Killing Leah and her mother was a no brainer; they hurt my baby girl and interfered in Bratva business. Mia on the other hand was a different matter. I knew Ella wouldn't want me to hurt Mia unless I needed to, so I just ran her out of town instead.

Dropping my bag at my feet in the living room, I look around, taking mental notes of all the things that I want to discuss with Ella about changing. Over the past few weeks, Ella has been telling me why she loved the house so much, and that's when I decided that I was going to give her this. The house that she grew up in will be the one that we raise our family in together.

I imagine Ella and I making dinner together as our children sit around the island telling us about their day. I can see us snuggling up in front of the fireplace as I fuck her.

My lips lift as all my ideas for the future play through my mind.

My phone vibrates in my hand, and I answer without looking at it. "Hello."

"Mikhail, I have news for you." My body stiffens at the voice. I should've checked my caller ID.

"Brendan. What do you have?"

"We found out who was recruiting among our ranks and stealing the weapons from us."

"Who?"

"It was Mallory Jones. She was a part of the German Mafia, but she is no longer a problem."

Relief fills my body. "Good to know. What do you need?"

"Nothing. I just wanted to let you know. I'm leaving, heading out west and taking Suri with me."

"Does Ella know?"

"Suri is going to be telling her later."

"Good."

The line goes dead and I put my phone away. Grabbing my bag, I head up to her room to get settled.

A few hours later, when Ella comes home from work, I greet her at the door. She gives me a huge smile. "What a surprise! What are you doing here?"

"I hope it's a good surprise," I say, kissing her on the cheek. I fucking love that she blushes from my touch.

Grabbing her hand, I lead us into the kitchen where I have a glass of wine waiting for her. Placing it in front of her, she looks at me through her beautiful lush lashes, "Mmm...I could get used to this."

"Good, I've been thinking since you won't move in with me at the penthouse. I'm going to move in here with you."

Ella sputters her wine as I finish speaking. "W...what?"

"I'm moving in here," I reiterate.

"No, it's too early. We haven't been dating long."

Cupping her face, I soften toward her, "Baby girl, it doesn't matter how long it's been. I know deep down you are it for me."

Her eyes glisten with the tears that she's holding back. My hand goes to brush the box I have in my pocket. Twitching to grab it and make her mine officially, but I know it's too soon. Her reaction was a sign, I need to be careful how I handle this.

A loud ring echoes around the room, we both look down and stare at the phone that's sitting on the counter. It's the hospital. Ella lets out a cute gasp, neither of us moving when Ella picks up her phone. "Hello."

I listen to her one-sided conversation and see the devastation and worry on her face.

"Okay, thank you, I will be there as soon as I can."

Ella hangs up. I can tell that the news isn't good. Her whole body is shaking as she tries to move frantically about the kitchen to gather her things.

"Ella," I call.

But she doesn't hear me. She keeps going, dropping stuff and muttering curses under her breath. "Shit."

When she goes to recover the keys she dropped, I stop her by wrapping my hand around her small wrist. "Ella, baby girl, talk to me."

Keeping her gaze down at the floor, she starts to speak. Her emotions have her in a choke hold but she still tries to push through. "T...that was the hospital, my dad isn't doing well. They want me to come see him."

She hiccups as I pull her up off the ground and slam her to my chest as I engulf her in my arms. Kissing the top of her forehead, I tell her, "It's okay. I'll take you."

When she pulls back, tears are streaming down her face, but she is so fucking strong. Keeping her head up, she nods and starts walking to the door.

I open the car door for her and when she plops down in the passenger seat, I grab the seat belt buckling her in.

When we pull up in front of the hospital, Ella doesn't even wait till the car is at a complete stop before she shoots out of her seat running through the doors. I let out an exasperated breath, as I place the car in park and follow her in, jogging to catch up with her.

I find her at the nurses station speaking to one of the nurses, who is looking at Ella with concern. I come up behind her placing my arm around her waist, trying to give her comfort and strength through my touch, not that she needs it.

"Hi. I'm looking for Marcus Thomas, one of the nurses called me."

"And your name?" the nurse asks as she types on the computer.

"Ella Thomas. I'm his daughter."

The nurse looks up at her with a look of concern, "Yes, Ms. Thomas. His room is 221. Down the hall and to the left."

Ella doesn't even slow down; she grips my arm and pulls me down the hall as she shouts back at the nurse, "Thank you."

When we enter, my eyes go to the thin, frail man lying in the bed with a thread bare gown covering him. Tubes surround him that are all connected to machines, each one beeping for a different reason.

Ella cautiously walks up to him. I can feel the sorrow and terror rolling off her. I hang in the back of the room, giving her the time that she needs with her father. I don't go too far though in case she needs me.

Leaning down, she whispers, "Hello, Papa. I'm sorry it's been so long since I've been here to visit."

She doesn't say anything else, just sits there as she rubs his arm with her hand, staring at him. Her eyes never leave him as the tears stream down her beautiful face. Fuck she's been crying alot lately.

I vow right then to make it my life mission to make her smile as much as possible.

Twenty-Two

Ella

No matter how hard I try, I can't seem to stop the tears from coming. I knew this day would come, I've been planning for it, but that doesn't make it easier. He looks so small, frail. He's not the same man I remember from when I was a little girl.

He was always a huge force in life. Pushing me on the swings at the park down the street from our house. Mother sitting on a picnic blanket watching us as we play together. How he would help me with my homework. Watching movies together to help take our minds off of things when mom got sick. Laughter and love surrounding us. Those days were the best ones of my childhood.

I'm lost in my head when the doctor comes in, "Ms. Thomas, like I said on the phone, his heart is failing. I think it's time to let him go.

We can give him medicine to make him comfortable as we turn the machines off. Do you have any questions?"

I hear him but I can't seem to focus on any particular words. I stay silent because I'm not sure there is to say anything. The doctor just waits patiently as he studies me. A large arm comes around and wraps around me, and I can feel his heat, his comfort. Leaning into my ear, he whispers in my ear, "Do you have any questions?"

Shaking my head, I'm able to squeak out, "No."

I don't dare look up though, I just keep my gaze on my father while I take the comfort that Mikahil gives me. But I can feel the doctors and nurses move about me as they do their job. Slowly the room goes from a cacophony of noises to dead silence and the silence hurts.

I don't dare leave. I can't leave him behind, no matter how hard I try, I can't hold it in. The pain. The loss. A sob breaks free and Mikhail holds me tighter. "He was the last of them. Now I'm all alone."

Mikhail turns my body to him leaning down to make us eye level. "Listen to me, Ella. You are not alone. You will never be alone. I love you, Ella, and you're my family now."

Hiccupping, I grip him, holding on to him as if he's my anchor and without him I would drift away. "What would I do without you," I whisper.

He puts his fingers beneath my chin, forcing me to look at him. The look in his eyes takes my breath away. "You will never have to find out."

We don't say anything else, turning back toward my father, embracing each other as he takes his last breath.

He was a good papa. Knowing it's time, I untangle myself from Mikhail, shuffling up toward my father's face.

It's easier to see his face now that he doesn't have any wires and masks covering it. We have the same eyes, the same nose and the same coloring. The last few years have been hard on both of us, but I'm glad he never knew the woman he married or how her and her daughters tried to destroy me and our memories. Leaning down, I give him a small kiss on his cheek. "Bye, Papa. Say hi to Mama for me."

I turn toward Mikhail, stand on my tiptoes and give him a chaste kiss. I whisper softly against his lips, "Let's go home."

Epilogue

Four Months Later

Standing at the windows of my penthouse, I look out over the city. We've been living here the last few months while her child home is being renovated. We are preparing it to raise our family in it one day. A sense of peace comes over me. My businesses are striving, my father and I are closer than ever, and I have Ella.

She changed everything for me and I have her to thank for all the goodness in my life. Footsteps start to echo down the hall. Speaking of the angel. She wraps her arms around my waist. "Mikhail, are you ready?"

I look down at the gorgeous woman by my side. Fuck, what is she wearing? Her body is wrapped in a luxurious black material that clings to every curve.

This woman.

Over the past few months, Ella has started looking more healthy. With who she referred to as the step-witches gone, she is lighter. And it shows.

The dark circles and the rundown look she seemed to wear has disappeared.

"If you keep looking at me like that, I'm not sure we'll make it to dinner."

I glance at the clock then give her my panty melting smile. "We have time."

I drop to my knees to pay homage to the goddess in front of me. Lifting up the hem of her dress, I grip her calf and lift her leg over my shoulder, opening her up to me.

Softly, I make my way up her thigh with my finger, teasing her. I graze against her panty covered pussy and fuck, she's so wet, I can feel it through the fabric. As I continue to lightly rub the outside of her pussy, she starts making her fucking sexy noises.

Her fingers tangle in my hair. "Do you like that, baby girl?"

"More, Daddy." She moans as her hand starts to tighten and pull. I love how she has started expressing herself more in the bedroom.

I smack her inner thigh. "Don't worry, baby girl, I'll give you what you need."

I slide her panties to the side and flatten my tongue as I lick her folds. "Fuck, you taste so good."

Flicking my tongue over her clit, I suck. She starts to grind her hips along my face as I continue to lick and suck her. "That's right, baby girl, ride Daddy's face."

"Oh, fuck Daddy. I'm about to come."

I let my teeth graze against her clit, and she fucking explodes on my face. I can't help but smile against her pussy and I don't stop, prolonging her orgasm.

Once she stills, I put her panties back in place then pull her dress back down. When I stand up, she throws her arms around me and kisses me deep not caring that she can taste herself on me.

"You are a beast, Mikhail, and I love you," she says as she pulls back.

I grin at her. "It's time to go to dinner."

"What about you?" she asks.

"We don't have time. But you can show me how grateful you are later," I say as I smack her ass.

***

When we pull up in front of the restaurant, we both step out and I hand my keys to the valet. Walking in through the front doors, her eyes go wide while her grip tightens on mine. "Mikhail, where is everyone?"

"I rented out the whole restaurant."

Stunned to silence, I turn her back to the young woman standing at the hostess stand, "Hello Mr. Sokolov, your table is ready."

We follow her hand in hand to our table and I pull out her chair. Ella, still silent, slowly and gracefully sits down. That's when I drop down on one knee and pull a ring out of my pocket.

She lets out an adorable gasp. Grabbing her hand, I say, "Ella, I have never met such a beautiful person inside and out. I want you to be my wife, my partner, the mother of my children. Ella, marry me."

I don't ask her, I tell her. Even she can't keep me away from her.

Blinking away tears as she looks at me, she gives me a soft smile. I know what she's going to say before she says it but the words mean everything to me. "Yes, I'll marry you."

Taking the ring out of the box, I place it on her finger. It fits her perfectly. A single modest blue sapphire in a platinum setting.

"I chose this ring because it reminded me of your dress the first night we met."

Before she can answer, I stand up, grab her face in my hands, and kiss the fuck out of her. Letting her know exactly how I feel. That's when all of our family and friends come out of the shadows.

"Congratulations!" they all yell.

As we greet everyone, accepting their compliments, I can't help but take in my fiancee. When we first met she had an air of sadness and a look of fear that had settled in her eyes. Now looking at her, the smile that she gives is the brightest I've ever seen from her. She seems lighter and brighter surrounded by the people who love her and that's all I've ever wanted to give her.

I step back allowing her to bask in all the love surrounding her.

A shadow comes up by side, I look over and find Zeev. "Congratulations, man. What does she see in you?"

"Fuck, I have no idea but I'm one lucky fucker that she does see something."

***

I hope you enjoyed Mikhail and Ella's story and will consider leaving a review. If you'd like a bonus scene of Midnight Blue click the link below for more!
Bonus Scene

Jake and Amber's story is up next in Golden Knight book 4 of the Twisted Grimm Series

Chapter 1

Amber

"Hey, Amber, did that order come in?" I turn around to see Max, the owner leaning over the bar. His slicked back, oily hair, looks as if it could be wrung out. A striped button-down shirt with the top three buttons open shows off his very hairy chest. I'm sure he thinks he looks good, but he doesn't. Not only does he look like a douche, but he grates on my nerves.

Unfortunately, I have to play nice if I want to keep being the manager of The Tower. And the manager of The Tower is the best job I've ever had and the only thing that feels right in my life. Well, except for the man in front of me. He never does anything for this place, he just gives me all his work.

Donning the most saccharine smile I can muster, I answer, "Yes the order did come in Max. I put it in the back."

Max's eyes don't leave mine. A shiver creeps down my spine as he checks me out and all I can think is *please leave*. I don't dare say a word either, I learned the hard way it only eggs him on. My prayers are answered because after a tense minute, he knocks against the bar. "Got it. Thanks, doll."

Turning away without another word, he heads toward the back room, to check his precious order. Knowing he orders supplies that are blatantly personal and not for the club pisses me off. Mocking him, I mutter under my breath, "Thanks doll."

He's such a patronizing asshole. Referring to me by some nickname that gives me the creeps. He doesn't talk that way to any of the male employees, just us women ones. *Aren't we lucky?* But since I'm the manager and interact with him the most, I hear it often. Too often.

"What a fucking douche," I say quietly.

The only reason this place is even remotely successful is because he was smart enough to hire me as the manager. But I suspect that Paul, who is the only man who has had my back these last few years, had something to do with it.

And speak of the devil. "Amber, are you good? I saw you talking to Max."

Paul is like a brother to me and the only one in this place who knows what happened to me in the past because he was there. He helped me to escape the nightmare of my childhood. I look at him with a soft smile, placing my hand on his forearm. "You worry too much about me. I'm okay. He was just being creepy like normal."

He nods but doesn't say much. He never does. But I know that he put Max on his list, the one he keeps for all the people who wronged him or those he cares about. When I see him settled at his post as bouncer at the door, I return to stocking the bar shelves, getting ready for the night.

Usually, Tuesday nights are slow, so I only put Mike on the bar, with me as a backup. Happy hour will be our busiest time today. I'm hoping to take advantage and get some paperwork done.

While I finish stocking shelves, a tall, dark-haired man comes in. He looks good but has an air about him. Eyes that are a deep brown but know light behind them. He stands tall in his fitted suit, and has a confident swagger about him that screams danger, and I've had enough of those in my life.

Putting on my customer service face I greet him. "Welcome. Feel free to find a seat anywhere and I'll be over to grab your drink order."

The man takes my cue without muttering a word and heads toward the booth that's in the back corner of the room. I watch him as he takes in his surroundings, checking to see where all the possible escape routes, hiding places and bad guys could be. Seriously, the man looks like he's an FBI agent or an armed robber. Once he's seated, I relax a tiny bit.

I turn back when the phone rings. "The Tower, Amber speaking."

"Amber, it's Mike. I'm so sorry but I won't be able to make it in today. I'm sick."

I glance up at the clock, and of course, he calls an hour before his shift starts. "Sorry to hear that Mike. Hope you feel better."

"Shit," I curse under my breath.

Mike not coming in today means I'm going to have to tend bar. There goes my chance to catch up on paperwork. But what can I do about it?

Not a damn thing.

Let's hope tonight is a slow night. Sighing, I put away the clipboard I was using grab my notepad, pen and head toward my only table. More people have joined him, but their backs are to me as I approach. Feeling the danger in the air, I keep my gaze down not wanting to peek anyone's interest at the table.

"Sorry to interrupt but what can I...." My voice trails off as I make eye contact with a man I haven't seen in a long time. Actually, I never thought I would see him again. What the hell is he doing here? I can't seem to look away, as I drown in his deep, brown eyes.

Someone clears their throat, I shake my head trying to clear the shock. When I go to open my mouth the only words that come out are, "I'm sorry...I can't."

I can't stay there any longer, so I run hoping that he doesn't follow me. I jog down the hallway toward my office but just as I reach the knob when a large hand closes on mine.

I don't dare look at him. If I look at him the walls that took me so long to build will fall and I need to protect myself, especially from him.

A deep growl comes from behind me. "Amber."

He sounds pissed at me, but I can't fathom why. I'm the one that endured.

I'm the one that was abandoned by everyone.

The one person I thought would come for me, never did.

Memories flood my mind; memories that I had buried long ago try to surface, but I can't let them. My heart starts to race. My palms feel wet and sticky. Trying to stay calm, I whisper, "Jake."

With his name on my lips, he spins me around. His eyes are swimming with rage. He slams his hands against the wall caging me. I stare into his eyes, trying to read his mind, understand his feelings. He dips his head down and growls in my ear, "Where have you been, sunshine?"

The nickname from long ago sends my body into a whirlwind. Goosebumps start to pebble my skin, my nipples spring to life, and my clit throbs. Shit. I didn't even think I had it in me for my body to react like this, it always felt broken.

Ignoring my body and him, my gaze darts up and down the hallway. I don't need or want anyone to hear this conversation. If Jake found me then the Wolves can find me too. Looking back up at him I try to turn to open the door. He relents and releases me, dropping his arms. I nod my head toward my office, "Let's talk in my office."

Also By Nichole Ruschelle

<u>Twisted Grimm Series</u>
Red (Red Riding Hood)
Green with Envy (The Frog Prince)
Midnight Blue (Cinderella)
Golden Knight Coming April 2024 (Rapunzel)

Acknowledgements

First, I want to thank my family. For being patient and allowing me to put in the work to get this book done, among getting ready for renovations. It was sometime stressful, but we did it!

Thank you to my friend and photographer Katie. Not only do you always have the best images for me to choose from for my covers, but I really appreciate you answering every voice message. Sitting through all me vents, and brain dumps during swim, while I made sure that I was writing the story I wanted to tell.

Karen thank you so much for taking the time to go through Mikhail and Ella's story. This one had so many moving parts I appreciate you keeping me on track and the storyline going.

Megan your proofreading skills are always helpful. I want to thank you for always doing it so fast too, especially when I'm so close to the wire.

Last but not least I want to thank all the influencers, reviewers, and readers for helping me spread the word about my books. Your love for romance books and wanting to share them with masses is amazing and the fact that you share mine means so much to me.

About the Author

Nichole Ruschelle lives in Texas with her husband, two daughters and her zoo of animals. She loves to write fairytale retellings where the prince of the story might not really be the prince, and the heroine isn't as helpless as some might think. In her free time Nichole can usually be found reading romance novels off of her Kindle. If she isn't reading, then she is usually found sitting at the pool or outside of pottery class while her kids do their activities.

STALK ME ON SOCIAL MEDIA:
Website: www.nicholeruschelle.com
Facebook Private Reader Group: Nichole's Romance Realm
IG: AuthorNichole Ruschelle
TikTok: AuthorNicholeRuschelle